Rubies - Text copyright © Emmy Ellis 2024
Cover Art by Emmy Ellis @ studioenp.com © 2024

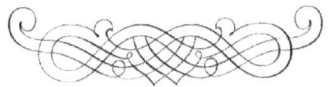

All Rights Reserved

Rubies is a work of fiction. All characters, places, and events are from the author's imagination. Any resemblance to persons, living or dead, events or places is purely coincidental.

The author respectfully recognises the use of any and all trademarks.

With the exception of quotes used in reviews, this book may not be reproduced or used in whole or in part by any means existing without written permission from the author.

Warning: The unauthorised reproduction or distribution of this copyrighted work is illegal. No part of this book may be scanned, uploaded, or distributed via the Internet or any other means, electronic or print, without the author's written permission.

RUBIES

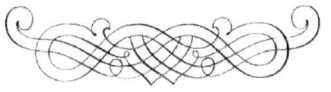

Emmy Ellis

Chapter One

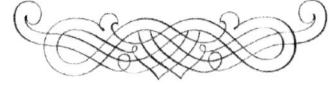

Nora Robbins paced her living room, waiting for her friend, Lucia, to turn up. Her muscles ached from all the tension. She'd ordered a Chinese, which would be delivered soon, and a bottle of white wine stood in the fridge, a notebook and pen on the dining table. They had a lot to discuss, mainly keeping themselves out of prison for a crime they'd been involved in years ago, at the same time risking going there anyway. No matter what they did, this could all go so horribly wrong. Nora sighed. Why had this happened *now*? Why couldn't *he* have just left them the hell alone? He'd brought the past back into roaring focus, and she hated him for it.

They had decisions to make.

A murder to commit—or another one in Nora's case.

Ever since the postcard from Clacton-on-Sea had arrived earlier, her anger had spiralled. Livid, she was, absolutely livid. The cheek of him. She knew damn well who'd sent it, even though he hadn't put his name at the bottom of the threatening message.

Just to rile herself up some more, she read it again.

> ENOUGH IS ENOUGH. I CAN'T LIVE LIKE THIS ANYMORE. THERE'S NO ONE LEFT I NEED TO KEEP THE SECRET FROM, SO I MAY AS WELL GO TO THE POLICE. IF YOU DON'T MAKE CONTACT BY THE END OF APRIL, I'LL TAKE IT YOU'RE PREPARED TO SERVE TIME FOR WHAT YOU DID.

Serve time? Not bloody likely. Why should they, when *he* was the one who'd set everything up? It was all his idea, a way to cover up what some in his family would call a sin, although these days most people were fine and dandy with that type of thing. Back then, though… She had to give it to him, he'd been in an awful predicament, and he'd needed money to pay off someone who'd discovered his secret. Laughable, she'd thought at the time, when he was loaded, but Nora had found out he didn't have much actual cash to hand, not enough for what he needed anyway. What he'd received had been governed by his father. That he lived in a big manor house was by the by. Appearances were deceptive, and while those on the outside looking in would think he'd lived a life of riches back then, they'd have been sorely mistaken, just like she had.

To be fair, Nora could have said no to the robbery she, Lucia, and two of their now-dead friends had done, but she'd needed money herself, which was generated from the sale of the jewels they'd stolen. All except the rubies, now lying in their black velvet bed inside a box in her safe. They had caught her eye the minute she'd spied them around his wife's neck long before they'd been stolen, and she'd coveted them, never thinking she'd actually own them. As well as a few other gems, she'd chosen them as her part of her payment, even though she knew damn well she couldn't sell them, nor could she wear them out in public. They were too distinctive, too well-known, in his family for generations. They'd featured in articles, something about them being a gift to his great-great-grandmother from royalty.

Looking back, Nora admitted her situation could have been solved another way—and God, she wished it had—but with the folly of youth, and in desperation, she'd panicked, taking the route he'd offered her. Instead of getting a loan from Ron Cardigan, she'd opted to go down a much easier route—funny how a robbery was easier, and less scary, than getting involved with Ron. And everything had gone well until the wife had put a spanner in the works.

And Nora had to get involved with Ron anyway.

She shuddered. *That* part of her past had been difficult to push to the back of her mind at first.

Ron had revolted her, but at the time, what could she have done? Backed into a corner—or, as it happened, against the wall—she'd agreed to do whatever he wanted.

The doorbell rang, and Nora jumped. It would be the dinner arriving, that was all, or maybe Lucia had got away from Dolly's Haven early, where she worked as a cook. The twins had created a refuge for domestic violence sufferers, a place for them to hide until George and Greg sorted their abusers. Nora wasn't supposed to know they owned it or were meting out their form of justice, but Lucia needed *someone* to talk to about the situation.

Nora opened the front door and smiled at the delivery man, the jolly one who was *so* jolly it got on her nerves. He handed her the bag, and she took it, saying thanks and hoping he didn't want to chat.

"Got company coming," he asked, "or are you having a feast all on your own?"

What the fuck business is it of yours? "Pardon?"

"The bag's got more tubs in it than usual."

That was the trouble, wasn't it? Other people gleaned things from your life by noticing the smallest things. It annoyed her—wasn't *anything* private? And now she was being forced to answer him when she didn't see why she should. Pre-postcard, she'd have barked at him to mind his own, but she couldn't draw any attention to herself by acting negative, not now.

She mustered up a smile "Oh, my friend's coming for dinner."

"Lovely. You have a good evening, Nora."

She should never have told him her name a few months ago, but at the time she hadn't been worried about needing to watch what she said in that sort of circumstance. If the police asked questions after the murder, he'd definitely remember she'd ordered extra food and was expecting company. As it usually did, her mind piped up, going to the dark side. It conjured the idea that he'd sit in his car and watch Lucia arriving. He'd make notes. He'd know they were up to something.

Stop it, you paranoid cow.

But she'd had to be paranoid in order to stay out of the nick. Granted, she'd let her guard down lately and had lived a relatively normal life free of the old worries that used to plague her on the daily, but since the postcard, she'd been reminded you couldn't become complacent.

"Have a good one yourself," she said and closed the door.

She stomped down the hallway and into the kitchen. Because of those plastic tubs the food came in these days, she couldn't pop them in the oven to keep warm. In her day, it was foil cartons—wasn't that better for saving the environment that everyone banged on about, or was foil bad, too? She placed it all in an insulated picnic bag and drew the zip across. Made a cuppa and sat at the little table, thinking.

Lucia lived at Haven and had also received a postcard saying exactly the same thing. It was a concern, that he knew where she now lived. For him to know she'd moved there, it meant he must have been keeping tabs on them. Nora had also kept an eye on *him*, although because many years had passed, she'd stupidly let herself relax more.

Maybe she should buy some tools from Amazon, the sort where she could take the rubies and diamonds out of their mounts in the necklace and matching earrings. Go to that dodgy bloke in Essex, if he was still alive, and sell them individually. It was the three pieces as a whole that would get her noticed as selling something she shouldn't have in her possession, but taken apart…that would work. It was better that she didn't have them in her safe anymore. Not now she was going to kill again. Her paranoia wasn't wrong on that score—if the police came, they'd find the jewellery and poke into her past. They'd *know*.

She took her phone out and browsed the online store, finding what she needed quickly. She popped it in her virtual basket, and the horrible thought entered her head that she was leaving a trail. Maybe she could make a big song and dance to him next door about a legitimate piece of jewellery she owned, a bracelet with cubic zirconia stones, saying she was going to turn it into a necklace instead, helped by a YouTube video. A new hobby. Old Roger was a bit of a gossip, and he'd spread the news up and down the street nicely. But, when push came to shove, would her purchasing those tools come across as a coincidence, like she hoped, or would it point the finger of guilt at her?

"Fucking hell."

She dithered on what to do.

"Sod it."

She bought the jewellery kit and prayed it wouldn't come to any coppers nosing in her phone history. Like she'd not long thought, who would think two ladies, one in her seventies, the other in her sixties, would go to the manor and kill a lord?

Because you used to work there, you silly bitch.

Nerves spiking, she shrieked at the doorbell going again. She'd have a heart attack at this rate. Back at the front door, she stared at Roger, wanting him to fuck right off. While she usually tolerated his visits, she didn't need his shit at the minute.

"I've got a problem with me tap," he said, brushing his snow-white fringe aside. "It won't turn off."

"Do I look like a plumber?"

Crestfallen, he wrung his hands. "It's just you know things. We don't call you the Oracle down here for nothing."

That was true. The residents usually came to her for advice. She'd engineered it that way. It made her feel special, wanted, but this evening, she didn't *want* to be fucking wanted.

She sighed and grabbed her keys from the telephone table. Roger led the way up his garden path and into the house, taking an age about it, so much so she had the urge to push him over so she could get past. The sound of running water hitting the base of his kitchen sink drew her around him and into that room. She twisted the tap.

The water stopped.

"Oh," Roger said, scratching his forehead, the gormless fucker.

Nora gritted her teeth. "Righty tighty, lefty loosey."

"What?" He gawped. Frowned.

God, give me strength... "That's how you remember which way to turn it. Right tightens it, as in shuts it off. Left loosens it, switching it on."

"But I did both ways, and nothing happened. It just kept gushing."

She glanced at his hands gnarled from arthritis. She ought to give him a break. It wasn't his fault she had jagged nerves for miles and had much more pressing issues to deal with than a running tap.

"Just remember the rhyme, all right?" she said.

"All right."

He repeated it over and over. The poor sod had gone a bit simple these last few years. With no family she could contact to let them know he might be having cognitive issues, all she could do was keep an eye on further deterioration, then phone his doctor about it when she felt he needed external help.

Selfish as it sounded, she didn't want to become his carer.

She strutted out, anxious Lucia had come and gone—Nora had left her mobile at her place so wouldn't have heard it ringing. But her friend stood on Nora's path, her phone held up as though she was about to call her.

"Oh, there you are," Lucia said. "I thought you'd done a runner."

Not for the first time, Nora acknowledged the differences between them were highly apparent. She'd succumbed to looking older, but Lucia, with her short trendy haircut, could pass for being in her fifties, not her sixties.

Nora closed Roger's door and skittered down his path and up hers. For a moment, she forgot she was supposed to have an issue with her hip. Sometimes, playing at being ancient to get sympathy went right out of her head. Her hip was fine and dandy, but no one needed to know that. It was Lucia who had a problem with hers.

"What were you in *there* for?" Lucia frowned and gestured to Roger's. "Did he have another problem?"

"His tap. Don't ask."

Inside Nora's, the door closed, they stared at each other in the hallway. It reminded Nora of years ago, during the robbery, when they'd done the same thing. The eye contact. The silent words. Suddenly Nora was young again, afraid of the consequences of her actions, of living with the guilt, and the recall sent a shiver up her spine.

"I've been that worried," Lucia whispered. "You know, about the postcards. What the hell?"

"I know. But we'll deal with him later. He'll soon find out he can't threaten us." Nora went into the kitchen, opened the thermal bag, and touched the Chinese tubs. Satisfied they were still warm enough, she put them on a tray to carry them into the dining room.

Lucia helped by getting the wine, glasses, plates, and cutlery. By the time they sat at the dining table at the front end of her living room, drinks poured, Nora felt a little better. Less stressed. Doing something proactive instead of fretting about it was always best for her.

They ate, chatting about where it had all started. Going through it to justify, yet again, what they'd done. But especially what *Nora* had done. This wasn't a new thing, they regularly regurgitated it, likely so she could remind herself it hadn't been her fault she'd killed people. But it had been *her* choice to pull that trigger, so why couldn't she face up to the truth? Why did she insist on blaming him?

Once again, for the millionth time, or that's what it felt like, Nora said, "Sorry I asked you to do the robbery with me. I was selfish. So bloody desperate. I'd say sorry to the others, too, but—"

"They're dead."

"Exactly."

Nora had often wondered about that—*how* they'd died and what it could mean. To have two friends pass away so tragically seemed off, but Lucia had said it was just bad luck, a coincidence. But what if *he'd* arranged their deaths? Had he also tried to come for Nora and Lucia but had failed?

"I think he tried to kill us," she blurted.

Lucia swallowed. "What? Not this again…"

"It's still bugging me after all this time. Think about it… If the robbers were out of the equation, his secret was even safer."

"Bloody hell! We've been over this umpteen times before."

"I know, but hear me out. You had that accident on the bus, remember. And that bloke who got into your house that time…if your Barry hadn't been in bed with you with his cricket bat to hand, think what could have happened." Nora was on a roll. "There was that near-miss with a car almost running me over, then that electric shock I had when I worked at the factory—it was proved someone tampered with that machine, just not who did it. And what about the man who dragged me down that alley? If I hadn't been saved, who knows what he could have done to me."

"But why would Quenton *stop* trying to get rid of us two? If he wanted us dead, he'd have carried on until we were, surely."

"We'll ask him."

Lucia nodded. "We'll need to do this carefully. Now I live at Haven, I've got Sharon and Hattie to worry about. The place is alarmed, so they're going to know I'm going in and out."

Sharon ran the place, and Hattie was the cleaner.

"We'll kill him over the weekend. If you cook stuff that can be heated up, there won't be a problem. You can't be expected to always be there. You're entitled to holidays—you work seven days a week, and come on, that's taking the piss. Say you're going to visit your sister. You can stay here instead, and we'll sneak out during the night."

"What about Roger? He's so nosy."

"Hmm, and there's his insomnia to think about, him standing at his bedroom window during the night."

Although Nora could bring up his mental decline as a reason for being 'confused' at what times they'd gone in and out, it was pointless. He forgot some things yet remembered others with staggering clarity. And when he did the latter, he recalled things with such conviction the police would likely believe him.

Nora had a brainwave. "What if we *both* put it about that we're going away? A weekend in Margate or something."

"But then we'd have to prove we were there."

"I'll book a caravan. We'll actually go there, get seen by the receptionist when she hands over the keys, then drive back to the manor Saturday evening."

"What about those cameras on the roads? They'll pick up either of our cars. Assuming we'll ever be suspected of killing him, that is, but we can't take chances. And me suddenly announcing I'm off on a jolly to Margate… Sharon will be fine about it, but the twins might get the huff that I left it until the last minute."

"I'll sort that, don't you worry."

"How?"

"The woman who manages Curls and Tongs, she'll give me their number. I'll speak to George and Greg, say it's for your birthday."

"But that's not until a fortnight."

Nora's temper frayed. "An early birthday present, then!"

"Okay."

"We have to do this," Nora said. "I'm not going to prison because Quenton fucking Goosemoor's decided to get us in the shit for something *he* organised."

Chapter Two

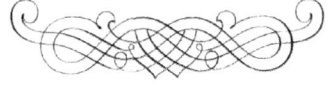

Nora hated her role as a maid at Goosemoor Manor. She cleaned, she ran around doing menial tasks, and Cook used her in the kitchen as the vegetable chopper, even though that wasn't in her job description. Quenton, her boss, didn't give a shit. The more he could squeeze out of the staff multitasking, the happier he was. Saving money was an obsession of his.

They said that, didn't they, that the rich hoarded their cash, they were stingy.

She reckoned he was around the same age as her, but they were worlds apart. Nora had grown up on a grubby East End housing estate where most people lived hand to mouth and gave you the clothes off their back if you needed them more. Quenton—or 'sir' as she was supposed to call him—had never known a second of poverty in his life, and if you needed clothes, he'd watch you walk round naked and laugh.

She despised him, the arrogant fucker.

Sometimes he watched her, following her around the manor when she did her chores. Maybe that was to keep her on her toes or he thought she was going to steal something, but it wasn't necessary. She took pride in her work—when that work wasn't pointless, like what she was doing now.

She stood dusting the ornaments in a curio cabinet situated in the foyer, a show-off piece of furniture that displayed a lot of wealth so those entering knew the score right away. As if the size of the manor wasn't enough confirmation that the family were nowhere near being on their uppers. Bragging was something Quenton liked doing, and passing on the stories of which royal family member, or peers of the realm, or famous people had given the family each trinket was one of his most boring habits. Unfortunately, visitors gasped and stared at the cabinet in awe, inflating his already insufferable ego.

The door to his large office to the right of the cabinet stood ajar. She'd been listening to him on the phone barking orders to the unfortunate sod on the other end of the line; he had no manners, and you'd think he would have because of who he was. Weren't lords supposed to be polite? He slammed the phone down loudly and swore. Nora got busy in case he stormed out and started on her; she wouldn't even be surprised, because his temper was legendary around here. He seemed uncomfortable in his own skin half the time, tetchy and moody. Sadly, Nora was usually in the firing line.

If she didn't need the job, she'd tell him where to stick it.

She used a toothbrush to get in the nooks and crannies of a bird ornament, although it didn't need cleaning as she'd only done it last week, and as the cabinet doors had seals, no dust could get in. Still, Quenton insisted it be done, and who was she to argue?

"Just a quick one," he whispered.
Nora paused. Why was he whispering?
She strained her ears.

"Yes, darling, I wish I could come, too, but Darcy's insisted we go to the charity function together... I know it's her thing and not mine, but I have to show willing for appearance's sake... Why do I have to stay married? You know *why. So no one suspects."*

Suspects what? Oh God, is he having an affair?

"Of course I love you!" Another whisper.

Despite him talking quietly, how stupid of him not to have closed the door. Then again, Darcy wasn't home and the children were at school, so maybe he thought the hired help would keep his secrets if they wanted to keep their jobs. That was the way of all things nobility versus peasants. It annoyed the shit out of her that she had to bow down to anybody, let alone those born with silver spoons in their mouths.

"I wish we could be open about it, too, but we can't... Please, stop going on about it. You said you wouldn't." A pause. "No, it's not something I can do. You knew that when we started. This was the deal: I stay married, and we meet whenever I can get away. You promised you wouldn't badger me about this anymore."

It sounded as if his bit on the side was getting tired of being the mistress. Was she pushing for him to leave Darcy? She clearly wanted more than he could give her.

20

"I have to go. We'll arrange something else soon."

Nora put the bird back in the cabinet and selected a solid-gold stag. She ran the toothbrush over its antlers and mulled over what she'd heard. Darcy was a cow, plain and simple, and if she found out about this she'd go mad, although she'd still stay with Quenton; being anything other than lady of the manor wouldn't suit her. Not to mention the shame if this news leaked. She'd keep it quiet, no doubt about it.

Nora was fucked if she would in the same situation.

Quenton came out of his office, head down in what appeared to be deep thought, and made for the front door. But he must have seen her in his peripheral; he halted, stared at her, and it was so clear he asked himself whether she'd overheard him or not. An expression of panic flitted over his pinched features, and he ran his tongue over his thick top lip.

Look at him in his fancy suit and expensive shoes. I could get a month's shopping for what they cost.

Nora tried her best not to be resentful, to be happy with her lot, but being surrounded by all this glamour made it difficult.

He studied her. "Good morning, Nicola."

"It's Nora."

"Right, Nora."

He strutted from the house, and the sound of his car roaring off meant he was going to see his father on the other side of the estate at Fotherington Gables. The same time every week, Quenton Senior orchestrated his son's life with commands and ideas, then Quenton came home and moaned about it to his wife, saying he wouldn't do as he was told—and ended up obeying anyway.

Nora finished the stag and inspected the other ornaments. They all appeared as clean as the ones she'd already done. No one would have a clue if she didn't polish the rest.

"Sod this."

She closed and locked the cabinet, pocketed the key in her apron, and took herself off round the back to have a cigarette. Cook had gone into town to the market, Patty the housekeeper was upstairs with another maid, taking down all the curtains for washing, and the other employees didn't give a stuff if someone sloped off. Those on the lower rungs of the employment ladder tended to cover for each other, the East End code embedded in them.

Nora sat on a stone bench in a walled enclosure used exclusively by the staff. Wisteria spanned the interior, creating a flowery, leafy oasis, and the June sun and clear-blue sky had her wishing she wasn't here but at home in her little patch of garden, a nice cup of tea to hand. What she wouldn't give for a day off.

She took her tobacco tin from her apron pocket and sparked up a premade rollie, and it wasn't long before her troubles overtook those of Quenton and his mistress. She was way behind on her rent, thanks to her husband, Oscar, who preferred spending it down the pub rather than handing over any housekeeping. He'd started doing that not long after they'd got married. Her job here paid enough to buy food and put money on the electric and gas meters, but the rent was Oscar's responsibility. The landlord had come round again last week, demanding it, and she'd asked how much they owed. The amount had shocked her senseless, and to top it off a collector arrived, stating Oscar had borrowed money at one of Ron Cardigan's poker games and the big man himself wanted it back.

She'd confronted her husband, which hadn't done any good. He didn't much care about anything these days apart from the pub and gambling. She'd asked herself whether it was her fault, his addictions. If she'd only been more exciting, he'd want to come home. If she didn't nag him so much, he'd want to spend time with her. But no, she'd been a lively and happy person when he'd made the decision to waste his money, so she wasn't about to take the blame. His answer to the debt problem was telling her to get a second job, and she had, cleaning in a pub seven mornings a week at ridiculous o'clock, but she wouldn't earn enough to pay the rent and Ron in the time she'd been given.

Part of her wanted to speak to Ron, tell him to do whatever he wanted with Oscar as the debt was his, not hers. But Ron was such a nasty bastard, she reckoned he'd say, even if he killed Oscar, that the debt now belonged to her. But she could try, couldn't she? Although if he refused to help, what the hell was she going to do?

The idea of stealing the stag came to mind, but Patty knew who was doing what at any given time, she even kept a ledger, and they had to sign their name beside each job at the end of the day. It wouldn't take long for the finger to be pointed at Nora if she nicked something. Getting rid of the stag wouldn't be a problem, there was that dodgy pawnbroker in Essex she could palm it off on, but what was the point in even entertaining that?

She smoked two rollies in all, then walked back to the house to hand the cabinet key to Patty and be told her next job. She had to go into Quenton's dressing room and put his laundry away, ensure all of his clothes hung in colour order, then tidy his drawers. She got on with it, leaving the drawers until last. She emptied the bottom one of socks so she could remove it and turn it upside down to get rid of any debris.

She stopped short. At the back, a cream envelope with his name on the front in capital letters. A quick glance at the dressing room door — it was closed — and she tugged the envelope free. Pulled out a letter. Should she read it? No. Was she going to? Yes. Because her mind had gone to the dark side, and if she had something on Quenton, he might just pay her the money she needed. Cruel of her, but with the threat of Ron getting on her back instead of Oscar's, she was desperate, and Quenton was loaded.

Dearest Quenton,

I can't stand for us to be apart. It's becoming harder and harder each day to hide what we have. I know what we're doing is considered wrong, and that to us it's perfectly right, but still, I wish we could be together properly. That things were different. I yearn for change, to be myself fully, but society won't allow it.

So forever, we hide.

The flowers are lovely today, the ones you planted. They've bloomed and turned their faces to the sun. The courtyard has never looked so pretty, but it would be prettier if you were here, sitting beside me.

Do you ever wonder what it would be like if the world could accept us together? It's a fantasy, I don't think it will ever happen, but those kinds of dreams keep me going. The hope that change is on the horizon, however distant it may be. Why can't we be like flowers, accepted for who we are?

Oh, how I wish we didn't have to hide like this.

I'm sorry, I keep going over the same thing time and time again. You'll leave me at this rate if I continue. I should do what you suggested and accept our situation and make the best of it. But it's unfair that Darcy gets to see you every day and I don't.

I'll stop this. Moaning about things we can't change isn't productive and leads to discontent, isn't that what you said? And it's true, I just need to remind myself more. Forgive me if I slip back into my maudlin ways. A gentle prod from you will set me on the right track.

I love you and always will.

Forever yours,

V

Sodding hell, was that Violet, Darcy's friend? A secretary, she worked at the same office as Quenton for the local MP. He offered his support there, too, both of them in voluntary positions. Or was V someone else? Call Nora suspicious, but reading between the lines, this woman could be a prostitute. Society would *frown on him for being with someone like that.*

Nora pondered the knowledge she'd gained. There was no way Quenton could say he wasn't having an affair because it was so obvious in those words, especially the declaration of love at the end. When did he go and plant flowers? And since when did he enjoy gardening? Chevvy, the elderly groundsman here, never got any help from the poncy lord who didn't like to get his hands dirty.

Nora placed the letter back in the envelope. She toyed with leaving it out on display for someone else to find—there was a small table holding all of his aftershaves, she could prop it between two bottles. He was stupid to have put the letter in a drawer in the first place when he knew his dressing room was reorganised monthly. He'd likely ask Patty who'd been given that job and come to Nora to see if she'd spotted the correspondence, accusing her of leaving it out for anyone to see.

She put the envelope in the drawer and continued with the contents of the next, his underpants, staggered to find yet another envelope. This one was white, and Quenton's full name and title had been typed on it. She opened it and unfolded the single page.

Lord Quenton Goosemoor,

It has come to my attention that you are of the other persuasion. How ghastly if anyone else should find out. If you do not want your secret to be revealed, respond to my request below, explaining what course of action you wish to take, although a little word of warning: saying no will result in dire consequences. Leave your answer under the front door mat outside your residence.

The request: I require the sum of five thousand pounds for my silence.

Cordially,

Mr Orchid

Nora let out a burst of laughter at the name—no way it was real. And that was a shocking amount of money. You could buy a whole house for ten thousand. Would Quenton have that sort of cash to hand? Of course he would. Had Quenton responded? And more importantly, if he'd done so, had Mr Orchid kept the secret? Or would more demands follow?

Nora now understood what V had meant. Of course they couldn't be together, it wasn't the done thing.

People weren't very accommodating over something like that. But if Quenton was a homosexual, had he married Darcy and had children to create an illusion? He must have.

"What do you think you're doing?"

The voice startled Nora, and she gasped, spun round, the letter still in hand. Quenton stood in the dressing room doorway, his face going pale. They stared at each other for such a long time it was awkward, so to break the tension, she spoke first.

"I want five hundred quid to keep my mouth shut."

He came in and closed the door, whispering, "I don't have it. I can't even pay that man! I have mere days to come up with the money, and I have no idea how to generate it. If I sell something in the house, Darcy will notice it's gone."

"I don't care. I've got two debts hanging over me, and I need the cash. Give me that stag in the curio cabinet. It stands at the back, so I doubt she'll see it's missing for ages."

"No, she checks them every morning."

"Then ask your dad for a loan."

"Are you insane?"

She folded her arms. "No. Most people ask their parents for help."

"Then ask yours!"

"I would, but they're dead."

He sighed. "I'm terribly sorry to hear that."

"I doubt it."

"Pardon?"

"You heard me."

It was strange to see him like this, all of his arrogance gone. It just went to show that even posh people had fears and emotions. She didn't feel sorry for him, though, not after the way he'd treated her over the years. She remembered every bark and slight, every condescending look. He deserved to be shitting bricks.

He took the letter from her and put it in the envelope. Popped it in the inside pocket of his suit jacket. "I'll burn this. I should never have kept it."

There must be another one somewhere if he knew he only had days to pay up. Where was it? In one of the other drawers? If he'd got rid of it, why keep the first one? It didn't make sense.

"Why did you?" she asked.

"I…I actually hid this one and forgot to dispose of it."

"Dangerous, considering I've just read it. I saw the other letter an' all," she said. "From V. I take it that's a bloke."

"Oh God…"

"Look, I don't care where you stick your dick, you're a haughty bastard either way, and it's rotten you can't be who you really are, but my main concern is getting the rent man and Ron Cardigan off my case, so—"

"You owe Cardigan?"

"No, my old man does, but whatever, I need five hundred quid. What have you thought of doing so far? You must have been working out ways to pay Mr Orchid."

"The only thing I can think of is a robbery, but I don't know who to trust, who to ask to do it." He paused. Eyed her. "Unless…"

She laughed. "Are you mucking me about? Me, rob you? Really? Patty would know. She's got eyes like a hawk."

"What if you came at night? Covered your face? If you brought others with you, it could work—it would look like an organised gang. I can give Patty the evening off, so it would only be me, Darcy, and the boys at home."

A thrill went through Nora but also a sharp slice of fear. That she was even considering this showed just how afraid she was of Ron turning on her and the landlord kicking them out, but could she pull it off?

"If I can convince someone to help me, I want more than five hundred. They'll need paying, too. And what

would we nick? We're not walking out of here with paintings, for fuck's sake, they're too big and heavy, and selling them on will be a problem."

"Darcy's jewellery."

Nora had polished it plenty of times. "But the set with the rubies, that's been in the newspaper. How the fuck are we expected to shift it?"

"You won't. Sell the other stuff."

"Oh, so we take all the risk while you just have a nice little chat to the insurance bloke, is that it?"

"Something like that. So long as I get five thousand as soon as possible, you can keep the rest. The insurance will pay out, so I won't be losing anything. I can't have this getting out, me and V. It would destroy me. Him. My father would cut me off. Please…this will be a mutually beneficial transaction."

She sighed. If it worked, she'd be well off for years if she was careful how she spent the money. No more worries about where the next penny was coming from. "If you can come up with a solid plan so nothing can go wrong, I'll think about it."

"Come and speak to me tomorrow. In my office at ten."

"The staff will talk."

"Not if I tell Patty I want you to dust all of my books and polish the shelves."

"Right. And just so you know, I knew you were having it away with someone before I saw the letter. You might want to close your office door when you're whispering on the phone." She glanced at the remaining drawers that needed to be dealt with. *"I'll leave the rest of that job to you and tell Patty you're letting me home early on account of me having a dicky tummy."*

She glared at him to dare the bastard to say no. But he didn't, so she walked out, smiling.

She'd played a blinder.

Chapter Three

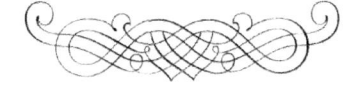

Switching the headlights off on the approach to Goosemoor Manor's driveway, Nora glanced into the distance at Fotherington Gables. Only one of the landing lights was on, so the tenants must have gone to bed. She'd worked there sometimes during spring cleans so knew the layout well. Quenton rented the property to some rich family who'd splashed themselves, and the interior pictures of the property, all over the local Facebook page. Bragging arseholes. They probably paid an exorbitant rent so Quenton could continue to live a life of luxury.

He'd appeared in the paper around a month after the robbery, insurance-payout time—like he couldn't have been more obvious he was spending it in a frenzy. The headlines claimed taking foreign holidays and having fun was a bit much, considering his wife and sons were dead. Another rag had speculated he'd gone off the rails, covering up his grief by filling his life with sun, sea, and booze. Then Quenton Senior and his wife had passed away within weeks of each other a month or so later, journalists saying they'd died of broken hearts because of losing their grandsons.

Nora coasted up the driveway. The drawing room light was on, so Quenton was probably reading or maybe even entertaining a boyfriend now he had no worries about hiding the truth.

Lucia breathed heavily beside her, sliding her hands into gloves like they'd discussed. It was all well and good saying they wouldn't touch anything, but it was best to safeguard themselves.

"Calm down," Nora said. "It's not like we're here to kill him tonight or anything."

"Stop it. I've been worrying all the way here that you'll lose your temper with him and do something stupid before we've made proper plans."

"What, like whack him round the head with one of his umbrellas?"

"Don't take the piss. This is serious. And there was no need to bring the umbrella up. I still feel so stupid about that."

Nora smiled at the memory from the robbery night and parked round the back beside the walled enclosure. She shut off the engine, darkness engulfing them. "God, the amount of times I used to sit in there and smoke my rollies. It's another world away. Where has the time gone?"

"I never thought we'd be coming back here. We said we wouldn't step foot on this land again."

"Yet here we are, all because the last of Quenton's family must have snuffed it so he doesn't mind his secret coming out now."

"Why would he care about what some ancient aunt thinks anyway? She was the only one left last time I checked. And in this day and age, no one's bothered about people being gay."

"I wouldn't be so sure about that."

"Well, they shouldn't be bothered, put it that way." Lucia paused. "And before I forget to say, I've read my postcard over and over. Something about what he put doesn't make sense."

"Like what?"

"He contradicts himself. He said he doesn't have to keep the secret so may as well go to the police, and in the next breath, he says if we don't make contact by the end of April, then we should be prepared to serve time."

"And?"

"Well, he implies if we *don't* meet up for a chat, then he'll go to the police—but if we *do* have a chat, he won't. It's the 'if' in: *if* we don't make contact. He's giving us an option. Why?"

"I get what you mean now, and no, it doesn't make sense. Especially because if he dobs us in, we're going to say he organised it all, so why would he put himself in that position of getting done for insurance fraud?"

"Which tells us he isn't going to the police at all. He just put that to scare us. He *wanted* us to come here."

"Fucker. I wonder what he wants?"

Lucia stared down at her lap. "The rubies? Is he spending too much and needs more cash?"

"He's not having them, they're mine. I've got plans for them, like you suggested years ago."

"What, taking them out of the mounts?"

"Yes."

"Why didn't you do that sooner?"

Nora squirmed. "You'll think I'm daft if I tell you."

"No I won't."

"Okay, they make me feel like I'm posh, same as Darcy. I wear them round the house and become a lady."

"Aww, bless you. Why get rid of them now, though?"

"I can't exactly have them in the house if the police come to ask about Quenton being dead, can I? They could dig into his past and see I worked for him. They'd have to follow it up, just so they'd crossed all the T's. Plus they're wasted in that safe. I've only got a limited amount of time left so I may as well enjoy it. The cash I'd get from the sale would help me do that."

"What are you going to do with it?"

"I don't need all of it, so we could split it in half. Go on holiday, a proper one, not just pretend to go to Margate. The Caribbean, something like that. A cruise."

"That would mean even more time off work. Why didn't you bloody well suggest doing this before I came out of retirement and moved into Haven? For God's sake, Nora!"

"Sorry."

Lucia huffed. "Come on, let's go and see what the silly bastard wants. And no letting him dictate to us, got it?"

"I have no intention of doing that." *This time.* She'd allowed him to influence her on the night of the robbery, she'd obeyed his commands, then lived to regret it. Who knew guilt was such a debilitating arsehole?

They got out of the car, Nora leading the way to the staff door that brought a slew of memories because it was exactly the same one, the same colour, too, although it must have been repainted over the years. She pulled the rope for the bell, one that used to get Patty scurrying to see who'd arrived, usually a food delivery or something for Darcy—clothes, shoes, perfumes. Patty had died years ago. Did Quenton have a live-in housekeeper now? That would make things difficult.

A light snapped on above the door, the glass case filthy, and she imagined Quenton or whoever peering at them through the peephole. How would they play this if someone else answered? Surely Quenton would usher them into his office out of the way.

Unless he's roped someone in on whatever he's playing at and they both threaten us.

She shivered.

Lucia linked her arm with Nora's, letting out a soft, "Shitting hell, this brings back some memories…" She took a deep breath.

"It does. Shame there's nothing we can nick this time."

Lucia chuckled. "You wouldn't…"

"Of course not."

The door opened, and a very different Quenton stood there compared to when he'd let them through this entrance on the night of the robbery. Old. Decrepit. Was that how people saw Nora? Ancient? He didn't appear shocked to see them, so he *must* have spied on them first, had maybe heard her car engine.

He stared at Lucia first, then Nora. "You're lucky it's a convenient time."

"You're lucky I don't punch your face in," Nora replied. "Are you alone?"

"Yes."

"What the *fuck* are you playing at? We agreed to forget what happened, not bring it up decades later. And what's all this about going to the ruddy police? Don't you realise we're not just going to take being arrested lying down? I've got a mouth, and I'll bloody open it, sing like a canary. If we're going to prison, then so are you. We'll say you forced us to do that robbery, you frightened us into it."

He glanced towards Fotherington. "Get inside, for goodness sake, you're being awfully loud."

"The Gables is too far away for anyone to hear us, and it looks like they're in bed, so stop being such a prat." Nora barged past him into the little stone-flagged corridor, flashes of the past assaulting her. Scrubbing that floor on her knees. Leaning on the wall to gossip to one of the other maids. Rushing up the passage to answer Darcy's summons. Fucking hell, she'd starred in her own version of *Downton Abbey*.

Nora breezed through to the foyer and took the top-left doorway into the drawing room at the front of the manor, mainly so she could see what Quenton had been doing prior to their arrival. As she'd suspected, the leopard hadn't changed his spots with regards to reading, something he'd done a lot of in the past. An open book, pages down, lay over the arm of his green wingback chair beside the fire which burned nicely behind the ornate metal screen. Everything was exactly the same except the wallpaper had changed from the dark maroon with gold fleur-de-lys to stark cream stripes alternating between shiny and matte. It certainly made the room look bigger.

She turned, Lucia coming in with Quenton close behind her. He gravitated to his chair, so Nora took the one opposite while Lucia opted to perch on the gaudy yellow chaise longue. Nora placed her gloved hands in her lap, Lucia following her lead.

"Were you telling the truth? No one else is here?" Nora asked.

Quenton lit a cigarette and inhaled deeply, as if them being there wouldn't stop him from enjoying a smoke. He exhaled, blowing the grey-white stream towards the ceiling, eyes closed.

"If you're trying to test my temper, don't bother," Nora said boredly. "We can sit here all night until you decide to tell us what the point of those postcards was."

"As I said, no one else is here. You can go and check if you want to."

"What about staff? Does anyone live in? Are they going to turn up any minute?"

"I live alone."

"So what's this all about?"

"You're going to do something for me, then we'll call it quits."

"Err, I don't appreciate you saying that like it's a given. And we were quits years ago. I seem to recall robbing your wife of her jewellery so you could pay off Mr Orchid."

Lucia snorted. "Mr *who*?"

Nora smiled at her, wanting to laugh. "I never did tell you why our lord here needed the money, did I."

Quenton held his cigarette midair and seemed shocked. "Pardon? You didn't tell your friends why?"

"You asked me not to, so I didn't," Nora said. "What's the problem? You don't look very well."

"I...uh...it doesn't matter. I'm just surprised, that's all."

"What, that I kept my word? Cheeky bastard. *Some* of us keep our promises, unlike you. If you did, we wouldn't be here now."

"Liar. You said no one would get hurt yet you shot my wife and the boys. Although I should be grateful. You did me a favour."

She shuddered at the word *favour*, preferring not to think about why it bothered her so much. "I see what you did there. Changing the past so it paints you in a better light. *You* said no one would get hurt, and you *ordered* me to shoot your wife and boys."

"That's how I remember it, too," Lucia said.

Quenton went on as if he hadn't heard them. "Hmm, a definite favour. No more having to sneak about behind her back and risk her finding out about me. As for those boys, they weren't even mine."

Nora couldn't believe what she was hearing. Was he rewriting the past again? "You what?"

He stared at the carpet, a flicker of emotion crossing his face. "Darcy had a man friend."

Nora would never have suspected the lady of the house had had an affair. "Really? Is that supposed to make me killing her all right, like she deserved it? I've beaten myself up for years thinking about what I did to her and those lads." She breathed through her nose, nostrils flaring. She had to change the subject before she got up and strangled him. "So you wrote us postcards, for what? What do you want us to do?"

"I have no one else to turn to, otherwise I'd ask someone else to do it."

"That old chestnut. I remember you said that to me before. Do you think I'm still like that dumb young girl I used to be? You *must* have someone else you can ask."

He tutted. "I actually don't. No one I can trust anyway. Look, none of us are getting any younger, and it may be ridiculous of me to ask you to kill someone but—"

"*Kill* someone? What the fuck are you on about? I've already killed three people"—*and organised someone else's murder*—"I don't want any more on my conscience." *Apart from yours.*

He tugged on his fag again, the lines above his top lip concertinaing. "I found out who Mr Orchid is recently. It came as quite a terrible shock, I have to say."

"I don't see the issue. He left you alone after you paid him off, didn't he?"

"Well, yes, in a sense, but…but he betrayed me in the worst way, and I'm afraid I can't forgive him for it."

"What did he do other than blackmail you?"

"I knew him all along."

Nora stuffed her hands beneath her armpits. God, she wanted to punch him. "Stop being so bloody cryptic and spit it out."

Quenton rose and walked over to her. He whispered in her ear, and she *supposed* she could understand why he wanted the man killed for doing what he had, but what was the point? Years had gone by, so what purpose would it serve other than for Quenton to get revenge? And was he even telling the truth? The man in question didn't seem the type.

He moved back to his chair.

Nora shook her head. "Listen, we're not killing him. He's too prominent. And besides, how would we even get him to meet us?"

"I'll ask him to come here."

"Oh, and he's going to keep that quiet, is he? Not likely. He'll have people he needs to tell regarding his whereabouts. He can't just swan off without anyone knowing. If he doesn't go home after his little trip here, people are going to put two and two together."

"But I can't *stand* it, knowing what he did. All those lies straight to my face. It's dastardly."

Nora couldn't hold back the burst of laughter at the word he'd used. "It's something you'll just have to live with. But if you can't, there's always The Brothers you could ask."

Quenton scoffed. "What, those dreadful twins? No, thank you."

"They're not dreadful, just a bit scary, but they'd get the job done, especially because the man lives on Cardigan turf, or he did the last I heard. Like you said, we're not spring chickens anymore. It's bloody stupid for us to bump him off at our age." *Although we'll give it a good go at killing you.* "Lucia's hips play her up anyway, so she's not going to be much cop."

"Yours is bad, too," Lucia said, indignant.

Nora ignored that, a flash of shame bothering her that she'd even lied to her friend about the hip pain. "*You* don't exactly look sprightly yourself, Quenton, so I can't see you holding him down for us."

He appeared hopeful. "Do you think they'll do it, then? What are their names? Geoff and Gordon?"

"George and Greg. If we keep our part in the robbery out of it, then maybe they'll consider it. You were blackmailed by a resident, albeit in Ron's day, but they still might want to right the wrong. On the other hand, they might tell you to go and fuck yourself because of who Mr Orchid is."

"Who are we talking about here?" Lucia said. "Sorry, but if I'm involved in this, I deserve to know the truth."

Nora glanced at Quenton who nodded.

"Mr Orchid is Ulysses King."

Lucia gawped. "What, the actor?"

"Yes, and the reason Quenton is so upset it's him is because—"

"Don't tell her that part." Quenton sucked on his cigarette then stubbed it out in an ashtray on a side table. "I can't bear to go through all that again, even if it's only talking to you two about it. Oh, the pain…"

"You dramatic bastard." Nora needed to get a question answered—she wasn't going forward until he put her mind at rest. "Before I even think about approaching those two nutters, I want an honest answer from you."

Quenton cringed. "What…"

"Did you arrange for Margo and Edie to be killed? Did you try to bump me and Lucia off an' all? What was it, an attempt to get rid of us so your secret was completely safe? You used us for the robbery then decided to get rid of us? What did you do when the attempts on us two weren't successful? Why did you just back off? And you said you had no one to ask to kill Ulysses, yet you must have used someone to get to Margo and Edie."

His face flushed, but it might not be from guilt. Maybe it was anger at her asking him such a thing.

"No, I didn't do anything of the sort."

He sounded like he'd told the truth, but she'd reserve judgement there. Maybe another request for the twins was that they got the truth out of him regarding that. Ever since Nora had thought about their near-misses and their friends' coincidental deaths, she'd wanted to know if he'd done it.

"Okay, I believe you. So are we agreed that I'll approach The Brothers, then?"

"That would be wonderful," Quenton said.

"And no more stupid-arse postcards and threats?" Nora stared at him. "We didn't appreciate that, considering what we did for you. I found it bloody rude actually. We put our freedom on the line just so you could hide who you are."

"Don't forget the five hundred you needed," he said, all snide. "It wasn't just me who was desperate."

Nora stood. "Don't get all pious with me, you fucking wanker. Yes, I needed money, but you needed it more than me. Five grand was a lot of money back then compared to five hundred, and think about the mess you'd have been in if your secret got out. Your dad would have packed you off somewhere out of the way."

"For God's sake, stop splitting hairs," Lucia said. "What's done is done. We all got a fair whack out of the robbery." She glanced at Quenton. "You didn't even have to buy the missus new jewels with the insurance payout because she was dead, then there was the life insurance you had on her and those boys—who we now find out weren't even yours. You pissed off abroad loads of times on those fancy holidays while we had to hide our wealth so we didn't get suspected, so no being holier than thou with us, it doesn't wash. The past is the past, and it stays there until George and Greg get told what King did."

Quenton nodded. Sighed. "All right. I apologise for getting you here on false pretences and worrying you. Mentioning the police was the only way I could think of where you'd take me seriously."

"Of course we'd take you seriously," Nora hissed at him. "We don't want to go to prison. Lucia would get about fifteen years for being part of an armed robbery, but I'd die in there because there's three counts of murder. Jesus, you really do only think about yourself, don't you."

"I'm sorry. Clean slate?"

Nora nodded. "It had better be."

She looked at Lucia who gave a tiny nod. So she was in agreement with Nora, then. They were going to kill him regardless. There was no trusting him now.

Chapter Four

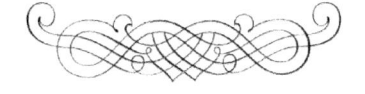

Nora didn't need a cane, but she used it in public. She'd grown crafty in the winter of her life, using her seventy-odd years to her advantage. The walking stick ensured she got a guaranteed seat on the bus, people getting up to offer her theirs, and help with the top shelf in Tesco, then there were things like George giving her that permanent discount on her cut and blow-dry.

Old didn't mean senile, but it got people feeling sorry for you.

She hobbled her way towards Curls and Tongs but didn't have to bother asking Stacey to get hold of the twins for her. A certain BMW sat at the kerb. Nora went inside the salon. George and Greg sat in chairs at the styling stations, chatting to two hairdressers. One customer had foil all over her head, reading her phone, and another sat at one of those nail bars.

Stacey looked her way from a sofa in the waiting area. "Blimey, back so soon?"

"I don't want my hair doing, it's those two I want to speak to." Nora waved her cane at The Brothers. "In private."

George stood. "Are you turning informant on us? It's fifty quid for low-level information, higher payments to be negotiated."

"Don't be ridiculous." The last thing she wanted was for Stacey and those two customers to think she was a grass. This information had to be kept top secret.

"Shall we go out the back?" Greg got up.

"If we have to," Nora grumped.

"Or we could go to the pub round the corner for a bit of lunch." George raised his eyebrows at her, clearly hoping to entice her so he could fill his belly.

Nora shook her head. "I wouldn't say no to free grub, but a pub isn't exactly private, is it. People round here are nosy bastards."

"A Chinese at yours, then?"

"I had one of those last night."

"Fuck me, Nora, can you be any more obstructive?" George glowered at her. "What do you suggest?"

"A ride in your BMW will do."

She followed Greg to the car, flapping her hand at George when he did the gentlemanly thing and tried to take her arm. "I can walk by myself, thank you."

"Christ, I was only being helpful."

"Yes, well…"

She got in the back and clipped her seat belt in. Greg sat in the driver's seat, and George climbed in beside her.

"What's with sitting next to me?" she barked, propping her cane between them. "Why can't you go up the front?"

"Because I don't want to have to crane my bastard neck to talk to you, that's why."

Greg eased away from the kerb, and Nora stared out of the side window at the scenery passing by.

"What's the problem?" George asked.

Nora turned her head to face him. "First, I need you to let Lucia have the weekend off. She works too hard, and I want to treat her to a couple of days in Margate for her birthday. All right, that's in two weeks' time, but whatever."

"Sorted. And second?"

"Second, I need you to kill someone."

George's laughter annoyed her. She supposed he saw her as a geriatric and thought her wanting someone dead shouldn't be a thing. He had a lot to learn. Yes, the numbers crept up with every birthday, but she felt much younger in her head most days. She only had the odd blip of the mind every now and then.

He ran a hand down his face and checked in with his brother in the rearview mirror.

"And who might that be?" he asked her.

"Now this is where you'll probably say no because of who he is, and I only just found out last night his significance in a good friend of mine's life, but all the same, he needs to die." *Good friend of mine. The things I have to do and say to get what I want.*

"Okay…"

"I'll tell you the story without mentioning his name first to see if you think his death is warranted—which it is. What I mean is, whether you'll take it on."

"Get on with it, then."

"Keep your hair on." She gave him a filthy look. "Years ago, I worked for Quenton Goosemoor at the manor. I was a maid. He was kind to me." *What a fucking liar you are, Nora Robbins.* "Always treated me fairly an' all that. Anyway, one night he got robbed. Four masked men broke into his place and nicked all his wife's jewellery—then one of them shot the wife and their little boys. Bloody dreadful, it was."

"Fuck me…"

"Hmm. Around that time, Quenton got a letter, and he confided in me." *He'd better appreciate all this bullshit I'm spouting.* "It was signed by some bloke calling himself Mr Orchid. He wanted five grand—that was a hell of a lot of money back then."

"What was the money for?"

"To keep a secret about Quenton."

"Which was?"

"That he's gay. I don't know the ins and outs of how it happened, but Quenton dropped the money off to this fella and that was the end of it. Until recently. Quenton found out who Mr Orchid is, and he's not happy. He wants revenge. This happened in Ron's day, and I appreciate you might not want to fix this when it isn't your issue, but Quenton is such a dear friend, and I wondered if you could help."

"Who's the Orchid bloke?"

"Ulysses King."

George's eyebrows shot up. "Jesus."

"I know."

He pinched his chin. "That could be tricky. He'll have bodyguards, I should imagine."

"That's the problem."

"It can be arranged, but we'd need to speak to Quenton first, make sure this is legit."

"Well, I believe him."

"You believing him and us believing him are two different things. We've got shit on the agenda for later today but could nip to the manor this evening for a chat."

"I'll let him know, shall I?"

"Yeah. I can't promise a time because we don't know if the job we've got on the go will take longer. Do you want to come with us?"

"What, to your job?"

"Fuck's sake. *No*, to Goosemoor."

When she got things arse backwards like that, it reminded her of how her mind wasn't firing on all cylinders at times. Yes, she definitely had blips. Like Roger. "Oh, right. Okay."

"We'll pick you up later, then."

"Give me a bell and I'll wait outside the salon, thanks. I don't want my neighbours seeing me with you." She gave him her number so he could put it in his phone.

He handed her a business card with theirs on it. "We're not that bad, are we?"

She stuffed the card in her pocket and would put it in her phone when she got a minute. "I don't want twenty questions, and my next-door neighbour's the worst of them. Roger's a nosy bark."

"Whatever. Right, it goes without saying that you keep your trap shut about our involvement. Otherwise—"

"I'm not stupid, I know exactly who you are. I watched you grow up, remember. Bloody ragamuffins."

George laughed. "'Ere, bruv, did you hear that? She wants our help but calls us names. She's still holding a grudge for when we plummed her house when we were kids. Reckons we're degenerates."

"You are," she said, smiling.

They dropped her off at the salon, and she ambled home. She walked up her garden path, cursing a blue streak—Roger opened his door and came over to the dividing fence.

"Don't tell me your tap's fucking you about again," she said.

"No, it's my oven. The inside light's gone on it."

"Then ask him up the road to fix it. Len."

Roger nodded. "I knew you'd know who to ask."

She fished her keys out and let herself in, leaving Roger standing there. She had too much going on to entertain him today.

Chapter Five

Now Nora had light at the end of the tunnel, she'd made up her mind to go and speak to Ron about Oscar, see where she stood in all this. She had to know if that bill was hers if Oscar refused to pay up. If the robbery went well and they were able to sell the jewellery, there'd be no problem, but actually, why should she *pay her husband's gambling debt?*

What was she really going to see Ron for?

The truth? She wanted Oscar dead. That was pretty drastic action, but he'd said he'd never leave her, and she believed him. She was his property, and he wasn't about to let her go. Plus he was a waste of space and treated her appallingly. What with Quenton doing the same, and her boss at the pub who looked down on her for being a skivvy, she'd had a bellyful of blokes telling her what to do and acting as if her needs and feelings didn't matter. Anyway, Oscar had thumped her the other day. Okay, she'd thumped him right back to get him to back off, but he'd still taken his anger out on her in the first place. One punch would lead to a thousand, and she wasn't standing for it.

The only way he'd stop was if he no longer breathed.

Her gut instinct in coming to The Eagle had been correct. Ron sat at a table holding court, his sidekick, Sam, sitting beside him. Five men around Ron laughed at something he said, and she resisted rolling her eyes at how they hung on his every word. Like he was God. Or was it because they were afraid of him and it was better the devil you know?

She caught his attention with a look and jerked her head towards the doors that led to the toilets. Would he come? Or would he ignore the silly little woman, thinking she wanted to plead her husband's case?

She didn't have to wait long. He pushed the door open and strode towards her down the corridor, his smug face showing that he knew this was something to do with Oscar. Of course, the man he'd sent to her door would have reported back that she'd been the one to open it. Would he be shocked at what she was going to ask him to do?

"In here." He opened a door and went into a room. "We don't want anyone knowing our business, do we."

Why had she thought he'd let her go in first? He wasn't a gentleman, so it wouldn't be in his playbook, and she cursed herself for being so naïve with her expectations. Ron and Oscar were built from the same mould, so she'd been daft to think she'd be treated nicely by the Estate leader.

She followed him, and he shut the door, locking it. That bothered her, being stuck in a room with him, but maybe this was so they wouldn't be disturbed. Glancing around, she gathered this was where Oscar had been playing poker as a table with baize on top sat in the middle, many chairs around it.

"What do you want?" Ron asked.

"I need to know what's what with the money Oscar owes you."

His eyebrows met in the middle. "What the fuck's it got to do with you?"

Relief poured into her, but should she trust it and lower her guard so quickly? "That's what I needed to know, whether it is anything to do with me. Your man came round asking for it, and I assumed…"

"Did you borrow it from me?"

"No."

"Then it isn't your problem."

"I thought…"

"Then you thought wrong on this occasion. If he doesn't pay his debt, I'll deal with him, so prepare yourself to become a widow." He cocked his head and studied her. "You don't seem bothered by that prospect."

She folded her arms. "Maybe because I'm not."

"Why?"

"Because he treats me like shit, that's why, and I'm sick of him."

Ron sniffed. "Maybe I should deal with him anyway, then. Because let's face it, he hasn't got the money to pay me back. Tell me you don't want him around, say the words."

She found she had no qualms, no second thoughts. "I wish he was dead. That good enough for you?" She shouldn't speak to him like that, he could get arsey, but she didn't like Ron and couldn't help herself.

He smiled. "You'll owe me."

"I thought so. What am I meant to do in return, then?"

He grinned, and it reminded her of a shark. She shivered.

"Let me fuck you against that wall right now, and all your Oscar worries will be over. No one will come calling for that money. The slate will be wiped clean."

She gawped at him, nauseated. Was he bloody serious? "What? You're married. You love your wife, everyone knows that."

"I do, but what she doesn't know won't hurt her. What other people don't know won't hurt them either, and if they find out I shagged you via that pretty little mouth of yours flapping, I'll deal with you an' all. I wouldn't bat an eye over shooting you in the face, understand?"

Fear pumped her blood faster. "Do I have a choice?"

"Not if you want me to sort your fella."

He came towards her, and she backed away until her shoulders hit the wall. He gripped her throat, squeezing enough to scare her; she couldn't take a big enough breath. He kissed her earlobe. Bit it. The backs of her eyes prickled from the pain. She hadn't given consent, but she supposed with Ron Cardigan you didn't have to. He'd take from you no matter what you said. She closed her eyes, hoping to get through this without crying, but when he lifted her skirt, she almost lost it. Almost said no. But he was going to 'deal with' Oscar, and that meant only one thing.

Death.

She shouldn't want that, but her hatred for her husband had grown so much, all she wanted to do was never see him again. Maybe Ron might banish him instead, but she couldn't see it happening. Oscar owed money, and the only result that could come out of that was paying it back or paying with his life. Ron might make an example of him, putting word about that he'd killed him. Others would think twice about borrowing money off him if they couldn't afford to give it back. Nora offering her husband up on a platter was doing Ron a favour.

He squeezed harder.

She bit her lip, him muttering that she could at least pretend she liked it, so as he entered her, she moaned and stroked his shoulders, holding back a gag. It was over sooner than she'd thought it would be, and he stepped away, zipped up, and went for the door. All so casual, as if he hadn't just done that to her.

He pointed a thick finger at her. "Remember, if you blab about this, you'll join Oscar."

She stifled a whimper, vulnerable with her skirt around her waist and her knickers uncomfortable where he'd shoved the gusset to one side. "I won't. I swear I won't."

"And act shocked when his body turns up, for fuck's sake."

"I will."

"Oh, and get an alibi for tonight."

Nora nodded. She'd ask her friends round, tell them about the robbery. They'd back her up when the police came. But fucking hell, Ron was going for it so soon? Maybe that was for the best, she wouldn't have time to think about it too much. She likely wouldn't even see Oscar today as he always went to the pub straight from work.

"Does he hit you?" Ron asked.

"Yes."

"Have you told anyone?"

"No."

"Then keep it that way. As far as Old Bill are concerned, you had a happy marriage. We don't want them poking into things and thinking you asked someone to bump your old boy off, do we."

"Right. Um, there's something else."

"What…"

"I need a gun."

Ron chuckled. *"And you think I'm just going to hand one over, do you? What do you want it for?"*

"I need to wave it about. There's this job I've been offered."

He scowled. *"Who the fuck's offered you a job that involves a shooter?"*

She needed that weapon, so she'd have to be honest. *"My boss at the manor."*

"Goosemoor? That dick?"

"Yes."

He frowned. *"Doing what?"*

"A robbery so he can claim on the insurance."

Ron outright belly laughed. *"You're fucking kidding me."*

"I'm not."

"What do you get out of it?"

"Money."

"What for?"

"Oscar hasn't been paying the rent."

Ron tutted. *"Christ almighty. When do you need the gun by?"*

"I'm seeing him tomorrow to discuss the final plan."

"Right, let me know what's what so we can arrange for you to pick it up, but now you owe me again."

Her heart sank. "Okay."

"I'll take what I want when you come to collect the gun."

"Fine." She wanted to cry.

He tilted his head. Stared at her. "What's your alibi going to be?"

"I haven't thought that far ahead yet. I've got to speak to my mates."

"You're roping them *in on it? You trust them that much?"*

She nodded. "They've always had my back."

"What are you stealing?"

"Jewellery. It's worth a shitload."

"All I can say is good luck."

He unlocked the door and buggered off. Nora straightened her skirt, repulsed by what had just happened against the wall, and leaned on it with her eyes closed. She stayed there for a bit, thinking that Ron now had something more to hang over her head—the robbery. And it was obvious he'd want sex for every favour he did for her.

She'd make sure she never asked him for anything else again after this.

Nora left the room, the nastiness between her legs a reminder of what had occurred. She went to the toilets to clean herself up then walked into the bar, head held high, and didn't glance over to where Ron had been sitting when she'd come in. He'd probably returned to his perch, thinking nothing of what he'd done. Standing beside Stanley, one of the regulars, Nora ordered a gin and tonic, needing something to steady her nerves.

Jack, the landlord, poured it and handed it over. "You all right, love?"

"I'm fine, thanks."

"Did something just happen?"

She frowned. "What do you mean?"

"It's just you went out there, then Ron followed."

"Did he? I was in the loo so wouldn't know. I had to leave work early—dicky tummy, see."

"Ah right."

She handed over the correct money and sipped, sinking onto a stool. Thank God she was on the pill, because Ron hadn't used protection. She tried to get her head around him wanting sex from her when he was supposedly devoted to his wife. What was that all about? And did he have sex with other women, too, telling them to keep it quiet? He held such sway around here and was so intimidating that no one would reveal his secret. He could do whatever he liked.

Nora pushed what they'd done out of her mind so she could pretend it hadn't happened, but it kept returning—his heavy breathing, the bite on her ear, his hand clamped against her throat.

She'd paid a man to kill her husband, just not with money.

Who had she become?

"It's okay to tell someone, you know," Stanley said quietly.

She swivelled on the stool to face him. "Tell someone what?"

"That you've got troubles. Seems like you've got the weight of them on your shoulders. I sit here a lot, studying people. I can tell when there's a problem."

"I'm all right, just tired. I'm working two jobs now."

"To pay for your husband's beer?"

"Err, no, to pay the rent because he spent too much on beer, get it right."

Stanley drummed his fingertips on the bar. "Same thing really. You're well shot of him if you ask me."

"Chance would be a fine thing."

"Hmm, his sort stick around when they've got a good thing going."

"A fool of a wife, you mean."

"And that. Still, accidents happen."

She gulped some vodka. "I don't know what you mean."

Stanley smiled. "There are people who've got your back, you know."

"I know."

"Thought you might."

He knew. He knew she'd spoken to Ron. He must be guessing about what they'd talked about, but he'd hit the nail on the head. She had to divert his thoughts elsewhere.

"If you're on about Ron, you couldn't be more wrong. Like I just told Jack, I was in the loo. And anyway, shouldn't you be more careful? If he hears you talking about him…"

"He doesn't bother me. I know too much."

She didn't press him to explain. All she wanted was to drink up, get home, and give her mates a ring. They could all do with a bit of cash, although none of them were the type to jump into a robbery. Nora would have to put forward her case, convince them it was easy money for the taking, get them thinking about all the nice things they could buy with their cut of the jewellery money.

She finished her drink and stood. "Right, best be off."

"Are you doing anything tonight?" Stanley asked.

"Just having a few friends round."

"Good, best you do."

Had Ron announced something about doing Oscar over to the whole pub when he'd come back from the poker room?

"Are you trying to tell me something?" She folded her lips over her teeth.

"Just to be careful."

Nora nodded and walked out, convinced the heat on the back of her neck was from Ron's stare and not the alcohol. She'd left her car at home after work so crossed the road and sat at the bus stop, catching sight of a poster on the side of the shelter. Job vacancies at the factory nearby. Rather than get the bus, she fished a mint imperial out of her bag and popped it in her mouth to disguise the fact she'd been drinking. She'd go and see if the owner would take her on, because there was no way she wanted to work at Goosemoor Manor after the robbery.

But what if leaving made her look suspicious?

She made her way to the factory and went into reception. "I've come about a job."

The woman behind the desk smiled. "We don't need anyone until the end of July, the writing about that is a bit small on the posters, but if you want an interview…"

"Yes, please."

"When are you free?"

"Now?"

"Oh, let me see if the boss is about. Take a seat."

Nora sat on a wooden chair and waited while the woman spoke on the phone. Prayed she'd be offered a position. Everyone moaned about the work here being repetitive, but it was better than cleaning that prick's manor, and she could give up the pub cleaning job, too. She reckoned the money from the sale of the jewels would be a lot, but she couldn't give up work altogether, it would look off.

"Please, God, make everything all right," she muttered.

"What was that?" the receptionist asked, putting the phone down.

Nora smiled. "Nothing."

"The boss will see you now. Just go through that door there, and he'll meet you."

Nora rose. If she got this job, everything would be rosy.

Chapter Six

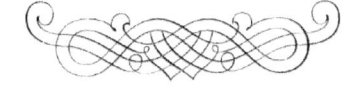

After leaving Nora, George had received a message from Diddy, one of the men who'd been stalking the abusive partners of the women at Haven. His brother, Kaiser, reminded George of himself—a little nuttier than his sidekick, a little more dangerous. George and Greg had met them through their sister, Stacey the hairdresser, and the men were a great addition to the team.

Greg drove home—the time had come to make a move on Morgan Nivens. His wife, Calista, and their children, Tasha and baby Archie, had lived at Haven for some time now. Calista had agreed that yes, Morgan needed to be taken out for what he'd done to her and Tasha—George's persuasion had made her see sense. But there was also the issue of several other men going 'missing' who just happened to be married to women at the refuge. It wouldn't take long for the police to twig something was iffy. It was too big of a coincidence for them to just brush that off.

We'll have to think about this a bit more. Work out how to play it.

Calista wasn't aware that today was the day her husband was going to be permanently removed from her life, but she would be soon. They'd pop to Haven and let her know once the deed was done. Morgan was going on the 'missing' list, not the murder list, and as Calista had left him, to all intents and purposes she'd have no idea he hadn't come home. That would be her reason for not reporting his absence, but his business partner, Shane, was bound to. The pigs would soon catch up with her once she'd moved out of Haven and her new address appeared in the system. She'd been coached on what to say, but what about the others? How would they get around that?

Maybe we could stage a multiple accident where their husbands all just happen to be in the same place at the same time when they die, and oh, what do you know, their wives live at a refuge together.

It sounded bad, didn't it?

George expressed his concerns to Greg as they dressed in forensic gear and slapped beards and wigs on. They stuck logos on the sides of their little van, one advertising holistic treatments, as usual a fake phone number beneath, a doctored number plate screwed on.

"That's a fucking big fly in the ointment," Greg said. "But what if we get them settled into their new flats first and registered on the electoral roll at those addresses, then the police will visit there and not Haven."

"We'll have to tell them to stay in the flats and put bodyguards outside until the blokes are dead. I'm not putting them at risk."

"Then that's what we'll do and hope for the best. If we spread the murders out over time, we'll be good to go. The issue is, Haven will always be open, so we'll always have abusers to kill. We can't bump *all* of them off and get away with it. Something to think about later."

Back on the road, Greg drove to the dentist where Morgan was currently getting treatment—a full set of veneers were being fitted, this information found out by Kaiser and Diddy overhearing Morgan bragging in a pub that he could afford to have them done in the UK rather than flying off to Turkey to get them done on the cheap.

Morgan owned a lucrative business, earned a lot of money, and lived in a massive house, which was in his name only. Calista had walked away from it all, realising the trappings of wealth weren't worth being beaten up over. George didn't blame her. The stories she'd told of the abuse she'd suffered—it was difficult for him to stomach and brought back memories of Richard, their fake father, hitting their mother. Add to that the trauma Tasha had experienced by watching her father punch, berate, and manipulate her mum, and it was a recipe that would lead to his death, because George and Greg knew damn well what witnessing that felt like. How it affected you into adulthood.

That poor little girl had been so jumpy and afraid when they'd first turned up at Haven. Thankfully, she'd come out of her shell, trusting George and calling him her uncle. She was more relaxed and slept with the Barbie *and* the doll's car he'd bought for her. She'd had to leave her other Barbie and toys behind in the rush to leave, so a new one had brightened her up.

Hopefully she'd be all right and wouldn't turn into a monster like George because of the trauma.

"Those teeth are going to be a waste of money," George said. "I'm going to knock every one of the fuckers out of his mouth one by one."

"I didn't expect anything less." Greg swerved into a parking space outside the dental surgery.

There was no need to worry about them being caught on CCTV. A camera operator on their books, Bennett, had conveniently switched the ones off in this area and would claim there'd been a fault in the equipment. They'd go back on once the van was no longer in sight. There might be eye witnesses to the abduction, but George wasn't bothered about that either. A quick word if anyone was brave enough to approach him, and people would know the score: back off or get kneecapped.

They sat and waited. George crunched on lemon sherbet sweets, Greg opting for a bag of carrot sticks he'd stuck in his pocket before they'd left their house. His eating habits had changed. He was on a health kick at the minute, suggested by his Dutch girlfriend, Ineke. Despite her meddling with Greg's diet, thus it having the effect where Greg badgered George to eat the same things, the woman was perfect for Greg. She had a busy life, too, so didn't moan that he couldn't see her much. She ran the girls for Debbie on the night shift on Kitchen Street, studied an online university course, and spent a couple of hours here and there investing money for George and Greg. The extra cash, when it grew to a substantial sum, was withdrawn and ploughed into Dolly's Haven.

"The amount of sugar you've just scoffed is shocking," Greg said.

"The amount of carrots you've had is shocking an' all. You'll turn orange if you're not careful."

"Behave."

"I'm not joking. People's skin does actually turn orange if you eat too many. Look it up on Google. There's pictures and everything."

"Nah, I'll take your word for it. Hold up, there he is."

Morgan came out of the building, took his phone out, and held it up.

"Taking a fucking selfie, the vain bastard," George muttered. "And look how unbothered he is about his wife and kids fucking off. It's like he doesn't care."

"He probably doesn't, other than she had the audacity to break free. Men like him think they own women."

Morgan smiled wide, his teeth ultra-bright, then shoved his phone in his pocket and walked down a right-hand street between the dentist's and a newsagent's. Out of the van, George led the way, jogging as quietly as he could, given his brick-shithouse size. Residential houses lined both sides of the road, but no one was about.

Morgan reached his car, a fancy Audi that likely cost about seventy grand straight off the production line. He blipped the locks and reached for the driver's-side door handle. George pounced. He whacked Morgan on the back of the head with the side of his fist, the bloke going down on his knees.

"What the f...?" Morgan glanced over his shoulder, eyes widening at the sight of two men in white outfits, one ginger, one blond. "Who are…?"

George gripped the back of the bloke's jacket and hauled him up. "Doesn't matter who we are, not yet. Now then, you're going to give me those keys so we can arrange for your posh-boy wagon to be taken somewhere to be destroyed."

That wasn't going to happen, it would be doctored and sold on abroad, but George loved the idea of Morgan pissing in his expensive underwear at the thought of a prized possession being ruined.

George held up a finger to stop the bloke's protests. "Uh, no complaining, that's not what you do when you're being abducted by us. Do you want to know what you do? You behave yourself, you do whatever we say, got it?"

Morgan swallowed and held up the keys. He could have easily stabbed one of them in George's face, but it seemed he was shitting himself sufficiently enough that he understood he really should do as he was told—or he was biding his time until he could leg it. George pressed the lock button then handed the keys to Greg who checked the street then bent to place them on the front wheel for Dwayne, their car thief, to collect.

George checked across the road. Dwayne peered out from behind a tree and waved. George laughed.

"What's the joke?" Morgan asked.

"None of your fucking business. Here's what's going to happen. We're going to walk nice and slow to our van around the corner, and you're going to get in the back as if you *really* want to. No fuss, no trouble." George smiled. "You're going to lie on your front and be absolutely fine with me tying your wrists together, and then we're going for a drive into the forest."

"The forest? What the hell?"

"Shut your mush. We just want a chat in private, that's all." A massive lie, but whatever.

George and Greg had agreed the cottage, given to them by their friend, Laundrette Lil, was the best place to take the abusive husbands. Morgan's dead body would be stored beneath. A steel-lined room, created by Ron Cardigan, had a trapdoor in the floor. Calista wasn't bothered about having to wait seven years for her husband to legally be declared dead. All she wanted was the peace of mind that she'd never bump into him again. She and the kids could then move into one of the twins' flats in the block they'd purchased, and Tasha could return to school. She'd been taught at Haven, a private tutor coming in daily now they'd found someone they could trust. They had no idea what would happen to the marital home, seeing as it wasn't in her name, but she didn't want it anyway.

"If it's money you want, I have plenty of it," Morgan said, his eyes darting about, him likely hoping to spot someone who'd help him.

"That's where you're shit out of luck, sunshine. We don't need your money. We've got more than you, but no one would know because we don't flaunt it. Our BMW is as old as the hills."

Morgan didn't appear to understand the BMW reference, a little clue as to who he was dealing with. "What…why are you doing this, then?"

George grinned. "All in good time."

He grabbed Morgan's upper arm and marched him round the corner. At the van, the bloke baulked, digging his heels against the pavement and opening his mouth, perhaps to call out for help. George twisted the prick's arm back and up, glad he'd hurt him—Morgan whimpered and gritted his teeth.

"What did my brother tell you?" Greg asked. "Do. As. You're. Told."

"All right, all right!"

Morgan allowed George to bundle him into the rear of the van, but he struggled from his grip and lashed out when George let go of his wrist to snatch up a cable tie from a nearby plastic box. George punched him right in his brand-new teeth, which must be extra painful because he'd only just had the buggers put in. Morgan howled and fell onto his back, but the knob still had some fight left in him. Just as he lifted his torso in an attempt to get upright, George picked up a rubber mallet and whacked him on the side of the head. Morgan flopped back down, groaning.

"You're getting on my wick." George flipped him over and secured his wrists behind him then sat on his arse. "Try and move now, I dare you."

Greg chuckled, shut the door, and got in the driver's seat. The van trundled off, Morgan's shoulders shaking. Was he laughing, the fucking maniac, or crying? George checked the side of the man's face, the other squashed against the floor. Tears pooled in the curve at the top of his nose.

"Bloody big baby. Now you know how Calista felt," George said. "It's not nice when you're bullied, is it?"

Morgan went still. "Calista?"

"Yeah, the wife you knocked seven bells out of on the regular. Remember her?"

"Where is she?"

"Somewhere safe, but she's understandably low on dosh. You're going to send her a hefty wedge for all the child support you haven't paid her since she had to run away. I'd say fifty grand should cover it—and I know you're good for it, we've had you checked out—but if you've got more hanging about, you can send her that an' all."

"Okay, okay, I'll do it. Then will you let me go?"

"Yeah." George wouldn't, he knew exactly what he was going to do to this fucktard, but he'd keep that to himself for now. "You're also going to send a text to her old phone—she's had it switched off ever since she came to us—saying what the money's for."

"Right, right."

Greg had been driving around all over the place so there wasn't a direct route from the dentist's to the cottage. He parked at the end of the street where Morgan lived so George could get Morgan to send the cash and text, then switch his mobile off. This would be registered as Morgan's last location when the police looked into his disappearance. George decided to write the message; an idea had sprung to mind on how Calista could clear herself of any involvement. It would mean ringing the police herself, but it could work.

MORGAN: THE LUMP SUM WE AGREED ON FOR CHILD SUPPORT HAS BEEN SENT. SORRY IT TOOK SO LONG. I'M SORRY FOR A LOT OF THINGS, TO BE HONEST. I HAVEN'T BEEN DOING WELL SINCE YOU LEFT WITH THE KIDS. I CAN'T APOLOGISE ENOUGH FOR THE WAY I TREATED YOU, AND IT'S HIT ME HARD, WHAT I DID. AS FOR THE NEXT SUPPORT PAYMENT, YOU'LL HAVE TO SPEAK TO SHANE. I WON'T BE AROUND TO GIVE IT TO YOU. I'VE GOT NOTHING LEFT TO LIVE FOR.

George hit SEND and switched the phone off. Gestured for Greg to get moving.

"What did you say to her?" Morgan asked. "You were writing for ages."

"Stop talking. I don't want to hear your whiny voice."

For the next few minutes, George relished the silence save for the hum of the engine. Greg turned down the track that led to the forest. He parked in front of the cottage and got out, opening the van's back door. George got off Morgan, climbed out, then pulled the man by his ankles, letting him flop face-first on the ground.

Morgan let out an "Oof!" then an "Ouch!"

"Be quiet, you fanny." George dragged him towards the cottage, no shits given that Morgan's cheek grazed against the concrete path.

I'm going to enjoy this.

Chapter Seven

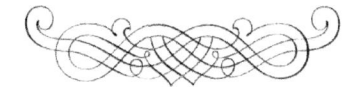

A naked Morgan hung from chains in the ceiling of the steel room, manacles digging into his wrists. Now George could reveal to Mr Nivens what was about to happen. Mind you, Morgan likely had a bloody good idea, considering they'd ordered him to strip and had strung him up.

"Why do you think you're here?" George wanted to see if Morgan would take responsibility for the results of his actions.

"I don't know. Honestly, I don't know."

"Are you thick?"

"Okay, maybe I do know. Something to do with Calista."

George reached up and patted him on the head. "There's a clever boy."

Morgan looked like he wanted to call him a condescending twat but thought better of it. "What did she do, send you to beat me up? Get you to force me to give her that money?"

"She sent us to do more than that." George smiled.

"What, then?"

"I'm going to kill you."

Morgan's eyes widened. "What? No! You're lying. She'd never ask someone to do that to me. Is that why she needed the money so she could pay you?"

"We do this shit for free when it comes to our residents."

George peeled his beard and wig off. Greg did the same.

Morgan paled. "Oh fuck."

George grinned. "So *now* you get it. I thought me mentioning the BMW was a big clue, but what do I know."

"Please, we can come to some agreement, can't we?"

"Not after what we've heard. All the shit you've done to her, what you let your little girl see? Nah."

"What did I do?"

"I see you're going down the route of making out you're innocent. That's okay, I'll jog your memory." George listed as much as he could remember from what Calista had told him. "Do you recall it all *now*?"

"She's a liar. I never laid a finger on her."

"How did she get those knife scars on her back, then?"

Morgan appeared startled for a moment then recovered. "She did it to herself."

"Really? Must have been a fucking long knife for her to reach all the way round there." George walked over to his little tool station in the corner and selected a slim-ended chisel and a hammer. He returned to Morgan. "Your stitchwork is shocking, by the way."

"What?"

"From where you sewed her up. You're crap with a needle and thread. Of course, you had to do it yourself because you couldn't risk her going to the hospital. There'd be questions. Do you know how *vile* it is that you fucked with her head so much that she *agreed* not to tell anyone? She's had to have therapy because of you."

Morgan paled. "Look, she asked for it, all right? If she didn't piss me off, I wouldn't have hurt her."

Why was that the standard answer for so many?

George glanced at Greg. "Hold him steady, will you?"

Greg went round the back and banded his arms around Morgan's torso. They'd only hung the bloke a foot off the floor, and with George's height, he was tall enough to be at eye level.

"Those new teeth of yours are going to find themselves on the floor." He paused. "Or down your throat, depending on whether you can spit them out faster than I can knock them loose."

Morgan glanced at the tools. "No, please…"

"You won't look so attractive when you're a gummy cunt, will you."

George lifted the chisel. Morgan shook his head, so Greg let him go and clamped a hand either side of it. Chisel lined up with one of the top-front veneers, George raised the hammer and whacked the end of the chisel handle. Morgan screamed, his arms flailing, the veneer shooting to the back of his mouth, blood pissing. A weird little upside-down triangular tooth hung loose, which was what the veneer must have been attached to. George tapped away at the rest of the top row until only a few molars were left. Morgan screeched with every one, blood and saliva draping over his chin in a sheet. He choked on blood, some of it spraying on George's face.

George smiled. Bored with tapping each individual tooth, this time he rested the flat side of the chisel blade against the whole bottom row and walloped. He dropped the tools and walked out, going to the kitchen, leaving Morgan to his wailing, which was fucking loud and annoying. He set the coffee machine on the go.

Greg wandered in. "He's gargling blood."

"Good. Want one of these?" He gestured to the machine.

"Yeah. We'll sit and have a break while he thinks about what he did." Greg sat at the little table. "Fucking prick. How long are you going to string it out for?"

"Dunno. I'm waiting for Mad to get in on the act." One of George's alters, the craziest side of him, the one who'd had to learn to know when to stop. In the past, Mad had just kept on and on until Greg pulled him off a victim. It had been a difficult time for George, admitting there were 'other people' inside him. Ruffian, the other one, had a Scottish accent and preferred scouring the streets alone, taking out random arseholes. Bloody weird how those two were entities all by themselves.

I reckon a doctor would say I need medication or sending to the funny farm.

Greg leaned back, stretching his legs out. "Think of Richard and Ron, that'll encourage Mad to come out. Our loser fathers always bring out the worst in you."

Barely anyone knew they had two dads—Ron the biological, Richard the surrogate, a man who'd hit George and their mother. Greg was right, the anger *had* ignited inside George now, his mind going back to the times when Richard had shouted in his face. When he'd fucked Mum's head up.

He let the fury percolate, drinking his coffee and dunking a few custard creams while he was at it. Greg gave him a look, all that sugar again, and George had to say something. Enough was enough.

"Listen to me, you. Stop either staring at what I'm eating to make a point or outright commenting on it. If you want to get all healthy, that's lovely for you, but don't expect me to do it an' all. If I want to shove Pot Noodles down my neck, I will. If I want to eat biscuits and sweets, I will. You do you, I'll do me, all right?"

"Don't moan to me when you get ill later on, then."

"I won't. I like your missus, but don't pass her suggestions about how to live onto me. I did just fine before she came along, thanks. You can go off people, you know."

Greg scowled. "Chill out, for fuck's sake."

Chill out? That was as bad as telling a woman to calm down. "No. You of all people should know I don't like being told what to do, so pack it in. Take your carrot sticks and shove them up your jacksie. *And* your porridge. It's the work of the fucking Devil."

"It fills you up so you don't keep snacking."

"I'd rather have a couple of bacon sarnies. *That* fills me up well enough. So are we clear?"

"What, that you want to eat crap? Yeah, we're clear."

"Good." If they had spats, they were usually forgotten a second later, and today was no exception. George had aired his gripe, and that was the end of it. "I've got a confession to make."

"Oh fuck. What?"

"I happened to say something in that text I sent for Morgan."

Greg turned away to lean his hands on the worktop, his head dipped, his back to George. "I swear to fucking God… What have you done?"

"He sort of confessed he was going to kill himself."

Greg spun round, eyes blazing. "Sort of?"

"Yeah. That way, Calista can make out she saw the money was in her account so she switched her phone on to see if he'd messaged her about it. She'll read what he said and ring the police. They'll do a welfare check at their house, see he isn't there, and once they can't find him, they'll assume he topped himself somewhere secluded."

"She's going to have to lie and everything. She's already been through a lot."

"She'd be spoken to anyway once Shane copped on that Morgan wasn't around, so she'd have lied regardless."

"I know, but this is extra pressure, getting her to call it in. You're an arsehole."

"I am, I don't dispute that, but I thought it was a good idea at the time."

"You didn't think it through. You should have run it by me first. Ineke's right, you basically rule Cardigan on your own. I'm just there to double the menace."

Now *that* pissed George off. "Been slagging me off to her, have you? What do you do, sit there and pull me to pieces on your dates? Fuck right off, bruv. That's hurt me, that has. Is she going to come between us? Because you know what I'll do to her if she does."

"Don't touch her." Greg glared at him.

George glared back, harder. "If she wrecks our relationship, she has to go. What about that promise we made as kids? You and me, no one can break us apart?"

Greg sighed and closed his eyes. "She said it as a joke, okay? Just an observation. It was more her taking the piss out of me for following you around like a dog."

"She actually said that, did she? Called you a fucking *dog*? That's not allowed. No one can say shit like that to you."

"Now don't go getting all protective…"

George's temper had risen to such a degree that he got up and went back into the steel room. Morgan became Ineke, and he laid into him, wanting to show her that if she thought he'd let her worm her way between him and Greg, planting little seeds, she had another think coming.

He'd watch her, watch the situation, see how it panned out, but if she ever, *ever* put another foot wrong…

I'll fucking have her whether Greg loves her or not.

Calista had taken the news better than Greg had thought she would. It seemed George had made the right decision after all, because she'd said she'd rather do it this way because it meant she didn't have to worry about the police turning up unannounced. She hadn't switched her old phone back on yet, she'd do it once the twins had left, but she was willing to lie through her teeth if it meant she could move into a flat with her kids sooner.

As far as the authorities were concerned, Sharon Turnbull was the face of Haven; no one, other than those who needed to be told, knew George and Greg funded it and owned the building. That meant no link could be made between them and Morgan saying he was going to kill himself. They'd hopefully take Morgan's text as gospel, do the required checks, then his file would sink into obscurity. Seven years down the line, and he'd be classed as dead.

On the way back from Haven, George stayed quiet. Greg accepted what George had said about Ineke, that no one was allowed to come between them—but what Greg *hadn't* told him was his girlfriend regularly passed on her observations regarding his brother. It was never done in a malicious way, so he hadn't taken offence on George's behalf like he usually would. Maybe she wanted to see if Greg knew the score—which he did, and he was fine with the way things worked—because she didn't want George mugging him off, but she didn't get the fact that it had always been like this. George had always led and Greg followed.

How could he explain to her that following his twin was what he'd always known? That standing in his shadow was safe and comforting? Being protected by George was a way of life, *their* way, and Greg also protected George by pointing out when he'd gone too far or explaining the pitfalls in any of his whacky plans.

Unfortunately, some of George's resentment towards Ineke had now filtered into Greg. He put himself in George's shoes, and if he heard some woman was chatting shit about him and George hadn't put a stop to it, he'd be livid.

Greg was going to have to tell her: no more snippets about her opinion on George. Greg had been blinded by his infatuation with her, he'd let their brother code slip by the wayside, and he had to make amends for that. Give it to her straight — that he'd never love her the way he loved his brother and she'd always come second.

"I'll have a word with Ineke," he said to break the tension.

George huffed and folded his arms. "Took you long enough to say you would."

"I'm sorry, all right? I didn't stop to think how you'd feel."

"No, you didn't. She doesn't understand us. No one could."

"No."

"So you'll *make* her understand?"

"Yeah."

"And if she does it again?"

"Then she's not the woman for me."

George relaxed, leaning forward to take a lemon sherbet from the glove box.

"Can you pass me one, please," Greg said.

"Thought you'd rather eat a carrot."

"Just give it to me, will you?" This was Greg's way of saying he'd also taken on board the fact that Ineke had put ideas about diets into his head and he was going against it.

A small win for George who opened a sweet and put it in Greg's mouth. "Was it me, or was Lucia jumpy when we spoke to her about letting her have the weekend off?"

Greg turned into their street. They had to burn the forensic suits and get changed. "She seemed surprised you'd agreed, that's all."

"Hmm, maybe."

Greg drove on towards their house, his mind switching from Morgan and Calista to Nora and their visit to the manor later. Killing Ulysses was all well and good, no skin off Greg's nose, but the bloke had an entourage they had to get around. This would need serious planning.

Greg shut the engine off in their garage. "How's Ulysses' murder going to work? Have you thought about it?"

"Not yet. We'll have a chat now over dinner."

"I'll make burgers and chips."

George raised his eyebrows. "What, no carrots?"

"Nah, I never want to see one of those again."

Chapter Eight

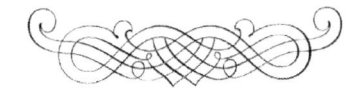

Nora sat at her dining table and looked around at her friends. Lucia sat opposite, her mouth dropping open that wide she was catching flies, her eyes rounded, cheeks going pink. Edie twirled a strand of long blonde hair around a finger, something she did when worried, and she also gawped at Nora. Margo

didn't seem so shocked, more contemplative, her black eyebrows beetling. She had the same dark bob as Nora.

"I take it what I said was a bit of a shock," Nora said.

"How can suggesting a robbery not be a fucking shock?" Edie snapped. "Bloody hell's bells. Are you out of your mind?"

"Maybe, but I'm also desperate."

"What the heck's gone on that you need five hundred quid?" Lucia asked. "If it wasn't so much we could have cobbled some together for you, but that's a steep amount."

"Oscar hasn't paid the rent for weeks, and he owes Ron a wedge."

Margo's eyebrows shot up. "Ron Cardigan?"

"Who else?" Nora said.

"It could have been Ron down the market. The veg man."

"I wish it was. And anyway, can you see Oscar shopping down the market?" Nora topped up their ciders. "Are you in or out? Just say if you don't think you can do it, then I'll find someone else or go there on my own."

"On your own?" Edie swiped the air with a flat hand, a firm no. "You said Quenton, his wife, and their kids will be there. How will you control all of them by *yourself and stop the missus going for the phone? And where are you getting the gun from you mentioned?"*

Nora's face grew hot. "About that…"

"Oh God." Margo gulped some of her cider. "Go on."

"Ron's lending me one. Not the veg man, before you ask."

"What?" Edie screeched. "I didn't know you knew him that well."

"I don't, I just asked."

"How much cash have you got to pay for it?"

No cash. I just paid with my dignity.

"Be careful with him," Lucia said before Nora could even answer. "Fuck all's free when it comes to that man. You watch, he'll pop up later down the line and say you owe him a favour."

Nora cringed. He'd asked for a favour all right. She prepared her lie. "He wants a necklace or something from the haul."

"How much jewellery is there?" Margo asked.

"Five necklace-and-earring sets, four other necklaces, eleven bracelets, twelve rings, and two tiaras. One of the sets can't be sold, though. It's the ruby and diamonds, the ones that've been in the newspaper. They're too well-known for us to flog them."

"She's been in the papers with diamond tiaras on. They'll also get noticed. What about taking the stones out of the mounts?" Lucia appeared to be coming round to the idea now the tally had been revealed. "And who are we selling it all to?"

Nora puffed air out. "There's that fella in Essex."

"What, Pinocchio Pawn?"

Nora smiled at that.

"His nickname says it all," Margo warned. "He lies about what shit's really worth and diddles you out of a proper payout."

"But he's discreet, sells it on to even more discreet people," Nora said, "and that's what we need. Losing a couple of thousand is better than being stuck with stuff we can't get rid of."

"True." Lucia tapped a fingernail against her glass, dislodging air bubbles that rose and popped on the surface. "What's the plan? How are we going to do this?"

"I need to speak to Quenton tomorrow. We'd need balaclavas, because I'm not going in there showing my face."

"Me neither," Edie said. "And where are we getting those from?"

Nora didn't want to, but she'd have to. "I'll ask Ron for some when I pick up the gun."

Edie pursed her lips at that. "What's our alibi?"

"We were round here having a get-together?" Nora suggested. "That's not unusual, we normally meet about once a month, sometimes more. That saves any of your husbands asking questions."

"What about yours?" Margo said.

"You and I both know he'll be down the pub. So long as we're back by eleven, we'll be golden and he'll be none the wiser. He can't stand us lot nagging anyway, so he'll go straight to bed." Nora wasn't brave enough to tell them that Oscar wouldn't be a problem by then. Her asking them to do a robbery was enough of a shock for one evening, and she didn't think they'd be able to handle knowing Ron was going to commit murder tonight. "So if Quenton's plan is solid, are you in? You all need the money, and think about how much we'd get each. This is life-changing."

"Yeah, but we can't go about spending it willy-nilly else people will notice," Lucia said. "It's not sitting right with me that I'd have to keep this from Barry. Say we got enough to live on for the rest of our lives — no, don't laugh, who knows what that jewellery's worth — I'd feel really bad for Barry going out to work every day, slogging his guts out, when he doesn't need to."

Panic burrowed into Nora's stomach. "We can't tell anyone. It has to stay between us and Quenton. And

Ron said he'd only help with the gun if we kept schtum." A lie, but she couldn't have these three swanning off to tell their old men what they were up to. *"Promise me you won't say fuck all. Ron won't like it, and he might do something to us. Bump us off."*

"Fucking hell, I'm not sure I want to do this," Edie said. *"Ron's bloody scary."*

"Then keep your gob shut," Margo said. *"We all buy extra stuff only on payday, we'll make out we've done overtime, whatever, but I reckon we should do it. Think about it, the manor is in the middle of nowhere. Yes, there's the Gables on the same land, but if we drive slowly so the engine isn't loud, no one will hear us from there."*

"God, who's car are we going to use?" Edie pinched her forehead.

"Mine," Nora offered. *"It's me who asked you to do this, so the least I can do is provide the transport. I can doctor the number plate with tape."*

"Why don't you sell it?" Edie asked. *"You'd get enough for the rent, then, wouldn't you?"*

Nora imagined getting the bus to work if she didn't have the car. Sod that. *"But I've already said I'll do the robbery…"*

Margo nodded. *"And that amount of money appeals. I get it. So where do we stand with Quenton?*

I mean, can we trust him not to turn us in afterwards?"

"He won't be an issue." Nora smiled. "I know things about him that he doesn't want getting out, trust me."

Lucia leaned forward, ever eager for gossip. "Like what?"

"I can't say. If he finds out I blabbed, the deal will be off."

A knock at the front door meant they all jumped, making it clearer they were on edge. Nora's stomach muscles cramped.

"Fucking hell, who's that?" Edie whispered.

Nora rolled her eyes. "Don't know. I don't have the ability to see through walls and doors, mate."

"Very funny." Edie glared at her. "You know damn well what I meant."

Nora got up. "I'll go and see."

She walked down the hallway, crapping herself. What if Ron hadn't had a chance to get to Oscar yet? What if her husband had got too drunk at the pub already and someone had brought him home? What if Ron then sent someone into this house tonight and killed Oscar while Nora slept? She didn't want to wake up and see the results. She'd prefer it if he was murdered elsewhere.

She opened the door.

Two local bobbies stood there.

Fuck. This was it.

"Er, yes?" she asked, acting the same way she always did with their sort, a dash of abrupt to her tone. Then she let her shoulders sag. "Bloody hell, what's he done? Has he got all lairy down the boozer? Did you have to nick him again?"

"Can we come in, love?" PC Ponce asked, real surname Partridge, but no one around here ever called him that.

Nora sighed. "Not really, I've got my mates here and I don't want them knowing my husband's a complete moron."

"It really is best we come in," PC Bell urged, glancing at his colleague as if silently apologising for butting in. "We can talk in another room to where your friends are if you like."

Nora tutted. "Sodding hell. Come on, then." She led them into the kitchen and closed the door. "What's all this about? It can't be anything other than something to do with Oscar because we all know what a pest he can be when he's had a few."

"He hasn't done anything this time. He was shot, Nora," Ponce said.

She stared at him. "What?"

"Someone walked straight into The Eagle and opened fire on him. Then they walked out."

She staggered to lean on the wall by the door. Shook her head as if in shock. She was, a bit, at someone just strutting in, shooting Oscar, then fucking off. Why hadn't it been done on his way home later? Where had Ron been? Had he done it? Or had he got someone else to, sitting on his perch and watching it happen?

"I don't…I don't understand."

A tap on the door startled her.

"Everything all right?" Edie called.

Nora's throat hurt. "No, it isn't."

"What's happened?"

Nora opened the door. "Oscar's been shot."

Edie's mouth formed an 'O'. "What? When?"

Nora turned to the officers for them to fill in the details. She allowed Edie to hug her.

Ponce took a deep breath. "An hour ago in The Eagle. Have you been here all evening, Nora?"

"What are you asking her that *for?" Edie blazed. "What, you think she shot her own fucking husband? Jesus Christ. Yes, we've been here all evening. Go and check with our other two mates. They're in the living room."*

PC Bell scooted past them.

"Who was it?" Nora asked Ponce.

"Witnesses say the shooter had a balaclava on, but by all accounts it was a man, going by the build. Did Oscar fall out with anyone?"

"Not that I know of. He's down the pub a lot, so you're better off asking people there. I don't mix with his crowd. Which hospital is he in?"

"Err, he isn't, he's still at the pub. I'm sorry to have to tell you he died at the scene."

Nora's legs went from under her. No faking her distress either. This was real, it had happened, and the enormity of it was staggering. Yes, she'd wanted this, but to actually face it… "Oh God, I'm going to be sick."

She dashed past Ponce and heaved over the sink—not somewhere she'd usually vomit, but it was that or the floor. Cider came up, and her stomach spasmed, sending another fountain out of her mouth. Someone rubbed her back, and she squeezed her eyes shut, thankful her friends had been here when she'd been told the news. Her alibi was set, and how horrible for that to be one of her first thoughts and not any pain Oscar had experienced.

"Was it quick?" she mumbled. "Did he suffer?"

"From seeing where he was shot, no. It would have been over inside seconds."

Nora remained bent over the sink. "Where…"

"Um, in the forehead."

"So it's someone who knows how to shoot," Edie said. *"Bleedin' 'eck."*

"Ron Cardigan was a witness, so it wasn't him," Ponce said. *"Just in case you were wondering."*

Nora rose and looked him in the eye. PC Bell, Margo, and Lucia crowded the doorway.

"Why would I wonder that?" Nora asked.

"Because many of us would. We all know who and what Ron is. What he's capable of. There could have been a grudge."

Nora shook her head. *"No, Oscar and Ron got on."*

Ponce nodded. *"Fair enough. Ron said the same thing."*

"There you go, then," Margo said. *"You'll have to look elsewhere, won't you."*

Ponce ignored her. *"Will you be okay, Nora?"*

"Yes, it's just been a shock, that's all."

"I'll stay with her overnight." Lucia planted her hands on her hips. *"My Barry won't mind sorting the kids."*

"Did Barry and Oscar get along?" Ponce enquired.

Lucia laughed. *"If you're suggesting Barry's the one who did it, it's highly unlikely. He can't even shoot his piss straight, let alone a gun."*

"And before you ask, my husband doesn't even know Oscar," Edie said.

"Nor mine." Margo folded her arms. "Whoever it was, it's sod all to do with any of us. Maybe he pissed someone off at work and they went after him."

Ponce nodded at Nora. "You'll be kept informed. We'll leave you be for now."

For now…

Edie showed them out. Nora, Margo, and Lucia stared at each other.

Edie came back. "Well, that solves the question of how to make sure Oscar doesn't open his mouth on the robbery night, then."

Margo and Lucia glared at her for saying something so crass in the circumstances, but Nora laughed. She laughed so hard she had to sit on the floor, her back against the sink unit.

"Fuck me," Edie muttered, "do you think she's losing her marbles?"

Nora sobered. "No, I'm fine. Absolutely bloody fine."

Margo frowned. "But your old man's dead, you can't *be* fine."

"Trust me. I'll be all right." She may as well admit it. "I hated him, you know, and I'm glad he's gone."

Edie got down and sat beside her, holding her hand. "What?"

"When he hit me, that was the last straw."

"Why didn't you ever tell us?"

"Because you lot have such good husbands. It was embarrassing."

"Aww, love." Margo crouched on the other side of Nora and placed a hand on her shoulder. "Sorry if you've been through the mill."

"I have, but it's over now. No more walking on eggshells." Nora sighed. "At least I'll be able to afford a funeral after the robbery."

The others laughed nervously.

"On a serious note, pay for it in instalments," Margo said. "We have to be careful."

"So you're all in, then?" Nora looked at them, receiving nods in return. "Let's finish that cider. I've got the rest of my life to celebrate as a single woman."

Chapter Nine

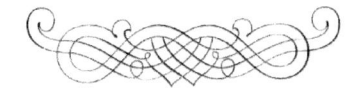

Nora stood outside the closed hair salon beneath a lamppost, her coat buttoned up to the top. It was a little nippy compared to recent days, but that wasn't a surprise. The weather was so interchangeable now. When she'd been a kid, there were distinct seasons, and she'd swear it hadn't rained as much.

Roger had come out just as she'd got to the bottom of her garden path, asking where she was going, emphasising and whispering, "In the dark…" as though to go anywhere then was against the law. She'd snapped at him to mind his own bloody business then walked off, anxious in case he spread gossip that she'd gone out at night when she usually didn't. Anxious in case someone saw her getting into the twins' BMW when they turned up.

Thank God she didn't have to worry any longer. It coasted down the street and stopped beside her. She got in the back, popped her cane next to her, pleased George was in the front passenger seat. No risk of him leaning towards her to ask questions. She'd found that annoying last time.

"All right, Nora?" he said.

"Not too bad, ta."

Greg drove off.

"Nervous?" George asked.

"Why would I be?" she barked.

"Fuck me, who put 50p in to wind you up? Think about it. You're going off with two known gangsters to discuss a murder. Most people would be on edge about that."

"I'm not most people. You two know what you're doing, so there's nothing to be nervous about. I'm just coming with you so I can be there for Quenton while you chat."

The rest of the journey went by in silence. Nora was chuffed about that. She had time to think through what she and Lucia were going to do to Quenton at the weekend. There was no gun from Ron this time, and using a knife would be too messy: they'd risk taking his blood home with them. Strangulation was out—it took too long, and she didn't know if her hands could suffer the strain. Maybe the gold stag would be poetic justice, seeing as he hadn't let her take it to clear her debts. It was heavy enough to make a dent, but there was the problem of blood again. Those antlers were bound to split his scalp.

We could whack him on the head with a rolling pin, knock him out, and hang him.

No, they couldn't. They weren't strong enough nowadays to haul him up—it would even have been a struggle years ago. Frustrated she couldn't find a good way to get rid of him, she almost blurted a question out: *How can two older ladies kill someone with minimal effort?* She thankfully stopped herself, though. Revealing to these two that she had another murder planned would likely get her a telling-off at the least and…she didn't want to think about what else might happen.

When the twins had been children, she'd had no trouble giving them a talking-to if they were naughty, her being the adult—albeit one they'd rudely stuck their fingers up at—but the tables had turned. Now *she* was the one who'd be in the shit if she stepped out of line. She hated feeling old, although being in your seventies wasn't considered old-old anymore. What she disliked most was being treated as if she was stupid just because she had wrinkles. Loads of people spoke to her like she was deaf, too, especially that bloody receptionist at the doctor's. "CAN. YOU. HEAR. ME. MRS. ROBBINS?" *Yes, you condescending little tart.*

But she had to face it, she wasn't the same age as when murder had last been committed at the manor, wasn't as agile or clear-minded. She couldn't stand there and dish out orders with the confidence and arrogance of youth. She couldn't leg it to the getaway car, she'd have to walk. Nothing was the same anymore, although Quenton looking and acting so old was to their advantage. He was frailer than them, couldn't put up as much of a fight.

Would he have pills they could force down his throat with alcohol?

The car turned onto the manor's driveway, and Nora glanced at the Gables. One light on upstairs. "Err, switch the headlights off?"

"No need. They're away, we checked," George said.

"How come the light's on, then?" Nora asked.

"Likely on a timer. They're in Poland and won't be back for another week."

Relieved she and Lucia didn't have to worry about that aspect, Nora sagged a bit against the seat. Then she tensed. Hoped Quenton twigged what she was up to when she made out they were best buddies in front of the twins. If he stuffed it up by questioning what she was saying… She'd have to get him into another room first and have a stern word.

"Let me speak to him on my own before you open your gobs," she said. "He'll be nervous because of who you are, even though he asked me to speak to you."

"Fair enough." George let out a whistle at the size of the building ahead. The drawing room light was on again but no others. "Before I forget to ask... Did you realise you'd made a mistake? That Lucia had?"

Her stomach rolled over. "What are you on about?"

"You asked us if Lucia could have the weekend off. I mean, why would we need to be asked that when Sharon's her boss?"

Nora cursed herself. Yet another thing to do with her age that she despised—not thinking straight sometimes, a touch of brain fog. Because of that, maybe she ought to confess about Quenton, let the twins deal with him if they thought it was the right thing to do, because what if she and Lucia fucked things up on Saturday night?

"I guessed," she said. "I mean, give me *some* credit. It's called *Dolly's* Haven, for fuck's sake. How many Dollys apart from your mum do you know? Sod all. I asked Lucia, and while she didn't tell me outright you owned it, her red cheeks told me I was right, so don't have a go at her, she didn't do anything wrong."

"It stands to reason you need to keep your trap shut."

"I've not told a soul, so *you* can shut *your* trap an' all."

George chuckled.

"Park round the back," she said to end *that* particular line of conversation. "You'll see a brick enclosure thingy."

Greg swerved around the side of the manor. "Does he know we're coming?"

Nora shrugged. "I didn't say fuck all to him. The way I see it, he's the one who wants Ulysses offed, so he can bloody well put up with us coming here unannounced."

"I like your style," George said, "but that's not a very nice way to treat your *mate*."

Shit, did he suspect she was lying about being buddies? Did he realise that a lord and his maid wouldn't have been friends?

She sniffed, scrabbling to think of what to say to cover her fuck-up. "Yeah, well, just because he's my mate, doesn't mean I have to give him the heads-up."

"Just thought it'd be the normal thing to do if you're besties, that's all."

Is he going to keep prodding the bloody ulcer? "Look, much as I like him, I'm missing my telly tonight because of this. It's got me a bit arsey, all right?"

"There's always catch-up, and you didn't have to come."

They got out, Nora relieved George hadn't dared to offer her assistance this time. She left her cane where it was—she hadn't used it when visiting Quenton last time as she hadn't wanted him to think she was doddery. She ambled over to the door to give the effect of a bad hip and tugged the bell rope, reminding herself she'd need to let Lucia know what excuse she'd given the twins about how she'd known they ran Haven—they had to get their stories straight.

She sensed the ragamuffins standing right behind her and imagined Quenton's face when he saw them. The door opened, light spilling out, and he nodded to Nora then raised his rheumy gaze to sweep it over the twins.

"Oh God, you came. Thank you, Nora," he said, all breathy and false. "Thank you *so* much."

She glared at him to rein in the enthusiasm. "I said I'd help. Let's go and have a chat on our own, then we can all see what's what."

Quenton shuffled down the corridor, his soft-soled slippers shushing on the stone floor. He stopped in the middle of the foyer. "If you two gentlemen would like to go into the drawing room…" He gestured towards it.

George and Greg headed off. Quenton led the way into his office and sat behind his desk, the leather chair creaking. Nora followed and shut the door.

"Listen," she said, lowering onto a nearby armchair, "I've told them we're good friends, right? They want to know your story before they make a decision. No saying anything about the robbery, got it? Well, not that it was me and my friends anyway. I told them why Mr Orchid blackmailed you, so you don't need to mention that if you don't want to. What they'll want to know is how Orchid's demand for money affected you over the years, plus how it floored you when you found out it was Ulysses. The more you can make them feel sorry for you, the more likely they'll kill him. This meeting is a persuasion tactic, okay?"

"Right."

"I mean it, if you so much as *hint* what went on in the past, my involvement…"

"I just want Ulysses gone, nothing more."

"You'd better not be lying. Come on."

They went into the drawing room. George and Greg stood by a bookshelf that held vinyl LPs which would likely fetch a good price these days. The old gramophone Nora had polished umpteen times sat on a nearby table. It had once belonged to Quenton's grandfather on his mother's side. The gold-coloured horn had gone dull where it hadn't been cleaned, a layer of dust smothering it. Shocking.

"Don't you have a cleaner anymore?" she asked.

Quenton nodded. "Yes, but she's not very good."

"I can see that."

Quenton sat in his chair, and Nora took the same seat as before. The twins turned to face them, so formidable that if she hadn't known them as kids she'd be scared of them. Yes, she was uneasy at the minute, what with the pair of them staring at her for whatever reason—to get the conversation going?—but as for worrying what they might do to her if they found out the truth… She'd stay true to form, clip them round the earhole and lie her way out of it.

"Quenton," she said. "Tell them what happened."

"It was such a dreadful, dreadful time…" He reached for a packet of cigarettes and played with it. "I was sent two letters by a man calling himself Mr Orchid, stating the sender knew…knew who I really was. He demanded five thousand pounds."

"What's the equivalent these days?" George asked. "Just so I get the gist of how much it actually was."

"Around forty-five thousand." Quenton took a fag out. "So as you can imagine, it's not an amount to easily get your hands on."

"But you must be rolling in it," George said.

"That's where you're wrong. Back then my father held the purse strings and only gave me so much. I couldn't go to him to ask for that amount as he'd have wanted to know why. How could I tell him I'm a homosexual? I couldn't. He would have disowned me." Quenton sighed.

"So where did you get the money from?"

"I staged a robbery so I could claim on the insurance."

"Quenton!" Nora shrieked. "It was *you*?"

"I'm so sorry, my dear, I thought it best you didn't know. I lied to everyone."

"Did you ask them to kill Darcy and the boys, too?"

"Good God, no."

"Hang on," George said. "Who did you get to do the robbery?"

Quenton drummed his fingertips on the arm of the chair. "I have no idea who they were. I spoke to…let's call him a nefarious gentleman…who set it all up. He and the robbers shared the proceeds of selling the stolen jewellery after giving me enough to pay off the person who wrote to me. None of them ever breathed a word, and they're all dead now."

George paced. "Right, so that's one thing we don't have to worry about. How did you find out Ulysses was Mr Orchid?"

"He confessed."

"What?" Nora sat up straighter. "So you've seen him? You didn't tell me that. When was this? It could mess things up, like the police knowing you saw him and they'll come knocking."

"I attended a charity ball—you know the one I mean, Darcy set it up years ago. He was there. He…he told me in the toilets. Said he needed the money to buy a house in case he was turfed out of the one his lover paid the rent on."

"So he was a kept bloke?" George clarified.

"Yes. It was as if he needed to get it off his chest, to come clean. He even said he could afford to pay me back ten times over now. For him to know I'm gay, I can only assume men talked back in the day, maybe one of the ones I'd slept with, and he found out. Used it against me. It was a few weeks after that he got his big break in acting. I remember it because it wasn't long after I buried my parents."

"I can see why you want him killed." Greg sat on the ugly chaise longue. "I'd be raging if I were you, especially if my wife and kids had copped it. I mean, if he hadn't blackmailed you, you wouldn't have set up the robbery and they wouldn't be dead."

"I'm quite aware of that, thank you."

Testy bastard.

Quenton lit his cigarette. Inhaled. "I may as well confess…"

Nora stared at him, but he wouldn't meet her eye. What the hell was he about to say?

"Confess *what*?" she said quietly. The last word had come out as a warning: *If you grass me up…*

He looked at her then at his lap. "It's hard to say it, but I need to get it off my chest. Their deaths didn't affect me like they should. I was emotionally detached from all three of them."

George frowned. "Why?"

"The boys weren't mine. My wife had a lover—and she knew I knew. I can't say I blame her as I found it difficult to…perform with a woman, as you can imagine, so she went elsewhere. All very discreet, of course. She wasn't one for caring about love and happy ever after, she just wanted to be a lady, and being married to me provided her with that title. There was no love lost between us—we played a part, acted as a united couple for the staff and our families, but it was a sham. My father adored her and gave her a generous stipend. She was better off than me in that respect. I went about my own business, you know, and she flitted off to a hotel whenever she wanted to see her lover. She produced heirs, so my father was happy. It worked for us."

"Did she know you're gay?" George asked.

"I didn't disclose that information to her, but she maybe guessed. I may not have loved her or the boys, they were more like houseguests, but for them to die…" He glanced at Nora.

"Terrible," she said. *But what you haven't told them is that I did you a favour. You didn't* care *they were dead, you fucking bastard.* She looked at George. "So will you help him? Ulysses' actions led to murder. It's ruddy awful."

George nodded. "Yeah, you've got a solid case here, but I'll warn you, Mr Goosemoor, we'll need confirmation from the man himself."

"That's fine. I have nothing to hide."

You bloody do.

"We need to get him on his own," Greg said, "away from whoever protects him, because he's bound to have a bodyguard."

Quenton tapped his cigarette against an ashtray. "I could ask him to come here without them. Not tell anyone."

"Why would he agree to that, though?" Nora asked.

Quenton gave them a wolfish grin, staring at each of them in turn. "Because I'll tell him I still have the letters he sent to me, which I don't, and mention that, who knows, fingerprints could still be lifted from it all these years later. DNA from him licking the glue on the envelopes and stamps."

George smiled. "Bloody perfect. Get him here for seven tomorrow night."

Chapter Ten

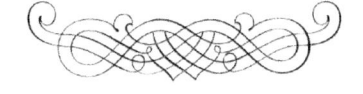

Quenton locked the back door once his visitors had left. He returned to the drawing room to pour himself a well-earned whiskey. He'd performed perfectly in front of those thugs, as had Nora, and his revenge would be complete come tomorrow night. He hadn't revealed the biggest issue to them, though, and thought perhaps he should. To George and Greg anyway, as they would be here waiting for Ulysses to turn up, and who knew whether the *other* secret would come to light. Ulysses was bound to blurt it under duress.

Ulysses, who'd always signed his letters as V. Ulysses, who'd continued his affair with Quenton after the robbery until some pretty little thing had come along and stolen him away, not to mention stardom. Quenton's heartbreak over that had lasted for *years*, and he'd had to mourn in silence with no one to offload to. All those holidays he'd taken him on soon after Nora and her friends had done the deed, all that money he'd spent on him. No other man had compared, and after their split, when Ulysses had made it as an actor, Quenton had gone to the cinema to obsess over him on the big screen—or Vincent Stubbs as he'd been previously known.

Quenton had thrust Vincent/Ulysses into the annals of time eventually, moving on, dallying with other men but never anything serious. He hadn't trusted anyone after that. Things made sense now the truth had come to light, and he'd worked out Vincent had lied to him well before becoming Mr Orchid. He'd blackmailed Quenton because he'd already been playing away behind his back and couldn't risk Quenton turning up at the townhouse and catching him at it with some twink. The house belonged to the Goosemoor family, a place where Quenton used to go, pre-Vincent, to have some space away from Darcy and her sons, and then later, when he'd become brave enough, he'd installed Vincent there.

He'd sold the house, unable to set foot in it again. Too many memories of times when he'd thought he'd had it all.

When he'd met Vincent, everything had changed. That man had become the love of his life, Quenton swept away by Vincent's youth (he was five years younger), his exuberance, the absolute joy with which he'd greeted each day.

The fun had gone out of Quenton's life once he'd been cast aside. He'd stupidly begged the man to take him back, but cruel laughter had been the only response. Quenton had drowned himself in more parties, more alcohol, more holidays in the sun, all on the insurance money, not to mention the life insurance paid out after Darcy's death, and everything had passed to him from his parents. He'd held a sale at the Gables, and the big house had become empty in no time, then he'd rented it out.

"What a dreadful man Vincent was," he muttered.

Time had a way of maturing you, and he looked back on who Vincent had been with revulsion. Quenton wasn't much better. The hurt had turned him bitter. Even before that he'd treated the staff at Goosemoor with utter disrespect, his arrogance what he was known for. He'd been so strong, so in control. He'd paid the children no mind, only tolerating them and their mother because they'd given him the cover he'd needed. Had he been young today, he could have come out as gay and proud, but that had been denied him in the old days, something he couldn't change, so there was no point lamenting over it.

Yet he still did. The unfairness of it. The wasted years.

He stared at the switched-off burner phone George had given to him. He wasn't quite ready to phone Ulysses yet, to hear the smugness in his tone before Quenton wiped it away with a few well-chosen words. He sipped his whiskey, smoked a cigarette, the mobile on his lap.

He could admit that wanting Ulysses dead because of the blackmail was a lie. Yes, the request for money had led to three deaths, plus two others years later, but the real reason he wanted him dead was the betrayal. The way Vincent had behaved when Quenton had told him about Mr Orchid's letter—shocked and disgusted some bastard would do that to him, all an act. The way Quenton was oblivious, still having sex with him, loving him, when all along, *Vincent* had been Mr Orchid. He'd kept the money Quenton had left in a paper bag in the men's toilets of a smelly, disgusting pub, take, take, taking from Quenton afterwards, still living in the townhouse until he was sure his new lover was worth giving up the old for.

"He used me. He never loved me at all."

His thoughts drifted to Edie and Margo. The 'nefarious gentleman' he'd mentioned to the twins had indeed been spoken to, but not about the robbery. And gentleman was being polite. He'd been a lowlife, someone who'd do anything for money and keep his mouth shut. Quenton had paid him to get rid of the women, making it look like accidents. A third party had been employed to do the actual deeds, and two drivers to mow one of them down, but the hits on Nora and Lucia hadn't worked. Then the lowlife had died of a sudden heart attack, and Quenton had no one else to ask to finish the task. He hadn't known who the third party or the drivers were.

Instead, he'd kept tabs on those two over the years—he'd have been stupid not to—but he'd known, deep down, they wouldn't reveal what they'd done, wouldn't get him into trouble with the law. How could they when they'd sold the jewellery on, benefitted from it, and Darcy and the boys were dead? It was a secret they'd be fools to pass on.

So he'd left them to their boring little lives, Nora a widow, Lucia busy looking after her two sons with her husband, Barry, becoming a widow herself when he'd died from a stroke at forty-one.

None of them had led particularly pleasant lives after that robbery. They'd all had crosses to bear. His anger had reared its ugly head when he'd typed those postcards on his old typewriter, but if he hadn't let that side of himself take over, he'd never have gone through with it. Nora and Lucia wouldn't have turned up at the back door and the twins wouldn't be killing Ulysses. Maybe he'd pay for this in the next life, but for this one, to be at peace, death needed to occur.

He picked up the phone and left the manor, driving to a built-up location, taking the exact route George had given him—something about CCTV cameras being switched off until midnight. In the quiet, narrow backstreet behind a row of houses, he turned the phone on and dialled the number from the business card Ulysses had slid into the front pocket of Quenton's suit jacket at the charity ball. Why had he done that? Did he want them to reconnect?

It rang three times.

"Yes?"

Vincent's voice enraged him. "It's me. Quenton."

"Ah, I knew you'd call. I saw it in your eyes. You still love me, don't you, despite what I did."

The assumption riled Quenton so much his cheeks grew hot, sweat breaking out on his forehead. "Sorry to disappoint, but I got over you many moons ago. You were nothing to me but a hole to fuck. I'm not ringing for anything other than to tell you a little story. Are you ready?"

Heavy breathing. *I've worried him.*

"Go on…"

"Once upon a time, a man called Vincent sent a man called Quenton two letters. Quenton kept those letters for decades, and once Vincent admitted to sending them, Quenton wondered about the advances in forensic technology. Fingerprints and DNA."

"You wouldn't…"

"Oh, I would."

"You'll ruin me."

"Like you ruined me. Come to the manor tomorrow night for seven—tell *no one* where you're going." He remembered what George had said just before they'd left. "*Don't* bring your phone. If you do, I'll out you to the press. After all, your luvvie friends and fans don't know you're gay, do they. It's Quenton's turn to blackmail Vincent. Goodbye."

He jabbed the END CALL button, switched the phone off, and smiled.

Checkmate.

Using his own phone, he rang the twins' number. Told them about Vincent being his ex-lover. With his conscience as clear as it needed to be, he lit up a cigarette and imagined how tomorrow night would go, then he drove the same route home.

Chapter Eleven

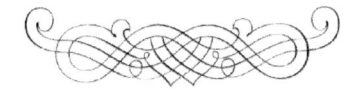

Nora, Lucia, Margo, and Edie had all squashed into Nora's little car. She'd left it in the street behind hers this afternoon, ready for them to sneak out of her house via the rear garden—less chance of her neighbours seeing them leaving, then. As it was summer, it wasn't dark yet, so no closed curtains, but

it had gone without a hitch—no one came along and spoke to them.

What if someone saw us, though?

"Where will we say we've been if someone clocked us leaving?" she asked, glancing in the rearview at Margo and Edie, then across to Lucia beside her. "That's the one thing we didn't talk about."

Margo swigged from a silver hip flask she'd filled with gin at Nora's. She'd been warned not to get drunk, that if she did she could become a liability, but clearly she hadn't listened. What the hell was wrong with her? Didn't she care that they'd all be in the shit if she made a drunken mistake?

Margo sniffed. "We'll say we nipped round mine for a bit. Julian's away, not due back for another three months. Thankfully, my *neighbours aren't nosy."*

Nora could have bit back her retort, but fuck that. "If you're so bothered about my neighbours, you could have offered to host our alibi at your house before now, but you didn't, so shut up."

Margo swigged from the flask again.

"Go easy on that stuff," Edie told her. "You'll be pissed as a fart by the time we go in, and that's not fair on the rest of us. We could all do with something to steady our nerves, but you don't see us going for it, do you?"

Margo grunted. "My nerves are shot, so leave off, all right?"

"Save it for when we come out," Lucia said. "I'll need some by then."

Nora parked in a lay-by near the manor so they could put their balaclavas and gloves on. "I can't work out if my gut's telling me it's going to go wrong or whether it's just normal nerves."

Ron's gun, in her jacket pocket, rested against her side. Just having it on her was enough to make her uneasy. She kept thinking it was going to go off and shoot her in the thigh, which was stupid. He'd loaded it, instructed her on how to use it, and she had to take it back tomorrow, granting him another hideous favour for the loan of the balaclavas. She dreaded it, especially when she had so much on her mind already. Oscar's murder, plus the robbery. She was going out of her mind, all the tension in her body making her snappy. And she still had to bury Oscar, an ordeal she didn't want to face. She'd have to cry, make out she gave a shit. Neighbours had been round, giving their condolences, but she wasn't stupid, they just wanted the inside scoop so they could go and gossip about it over a drink down the pub.

Roger had been good, though. He'd given her space for once and told her she knew where he was if she needed him. His wife had died early in their marriage, and he hadn't been with anyone since. Would Nora be the same?

"Maybe we should back out," Margo said. "Let Quenton deal with it another way. It's not our problem some nutter sent him a creepy letter."

Nora gritted her teeth. "We could if I didn't need the rent money. If you can find the cash for me some other way, be my guest, but we've already established you can't. And like I said before, I've already agreed to do it."

"You're acting like the rent's **our** fault and we have **to do this. It's your** debt."

Didn't they say people always spoke the truth when they'd had a drink?

"It was Oscar's bleedin' fault," Lucia said. "Nora's our mate, and she'd do the same for us if it was the other way round. And shut up before you say something you'll regret."

Nora appreciated the support, she'd always been closer to Lucia than the other two, but her mind was already elsewhere. Another thing weighed heavy. She was the one who'd go and see Pinocchio Pawn in Essex. There was no time to wait for the fallout from the robbery to die down—Nora and Quenton needed the money quickly, so she had to get rid of the jewellery as soon as possible. But what if Pinocchio wouldn't buy it? What if he heard about the robbery on the news in the morning and guessed where she'd got the gear from? He might tell the police.

"I'm so sorry for dragging you all into this, but if I don't pay the landlord, I'll be chucked out by the end of the month." Nora let out a long breath. Now she didn't have to pay Ron back, she didn't need five hundred anymore, but between them, they still wouldn't be able to cobble together enough for the rent arrears. "I'll never forget you for helping me, I promise. Let's just get on with it. We need to be back by eleven so you can all go home as usual."

"Like nothing happened?" Margo said. "That's a joke. This will change us forever."

"You could have said no," Lucia snapped. "We all could."

"And it's not like you're not getting paid," Edie reminded her. "You'll be debt-free, and you can open that shop you're always going on about. It won't be just a dream anymore. I'm going to leave my job and get myself a market stall. I've been planning it in my head for years but didn't have the money to buy the stock. We'll all *be better off."*

Nora started the engine and drove on. "If you want to back out, Margo, sit in the car until we've finished.

You can have a bracelet or something for coming this far."

"Ignore me. I'm just worried."

"We all are," Edie said. *"God, it's always about you, isn't it."*

"Piss off," Margo huffed.

"Pack it in now." Nora veered up the driveway, her heartbeat erratic. Her mates arguing, on top of the stress pre-robbery, was making things worse, and now she felt guilty because Margo clearly had the hump about why they were doing this.

Why the fuck did she agree then? Wasn't she the one who'd prompted the other two to do this?

Nora focused on the house to stop herself from asking those questions—Margo might not want to admit she was as desperate to move up the ladder in life as the rest of them. If things had gone to plan, Darcy was putting the kids to bed, seeing as Patty had been sent home early. But what if she'd forgotten something and came back right in the middle of the robbery?

Fucking hell.

Nora parked by the walled enclosure, turning to point the car towards the way out for a quicker getaway. What if Darcy had heard the car and came to nose out of the back window? Nora glanced across at the Gables—it was about eight o'clock, so Quenton Senior and his wife wouldn't have gone to bed yet. The risk tonight was so great, and so much could go wrong. Senior could take it upon himself to drive over in his Range Rover for a chat. Or Darcy might not do as she was told. There was the gun for threatening her with, but she still might not comply. She wasn't exactly the wallflower type and regularly barked at the staff if things weren't to her liking. Nora had gone through everything with Quenton, and she'd relayed it to her friends, obviously, but just because it was written in stone for them, it might not turn out that way in reality.

Darcy and the boys were the sticking point. What they did—or didn't do—would determine whether the outcome was different to the plan.

"Come on, let's do this." She'd said this more to herself than her mates. A little pep talk.

She got out, praying the others remembered the floor plan she'd drawn for them to study so they were aware of the four exits: two at the back, one at the side, the other at the front. She waited for them to join her at the tradesman's entrance, then pointed to the left at the French doors in the main sitting room.

"Ready?" she whispered.

They nodded. The sight of them in balaclavas, the skin around their eyes pale holes in the black wool, gave Nora the creeps. She turned away to tap on the door instead of pulling the bell rope, as per Quenton's instructions. Again Nora checked the Gables—no headlights coming their way—her attention drawn back to the door as it opened.

Quenton must have been loitering behind it after he'd heard her car engine. "She's upstairs reading a story to the boys. They're playing her up because Patty usually does the bedtime routine before she goes home. Give it two minutes, then come in." He left the door wide open and strutted down the corridor towards the foyer. He'd wait for them in the sitting room.

Lucia came forward to stand next to Nora. "Bloody hell, mate, he's well posh…"

"He still shits brown," Edie said behind them.

Margo giggled—bloody hell, the booze must have affected her.

Nora glanced over her shoulder. "This isn't a fucking joke."

"Sorry." Margo dipped her head.

"This is as serious as it gets for us," Nora warned. "If we're caught…"

"Oh, don't," Edie said. "I'm worried enough as it is."

"Have two minutes gone past yet?" Lucia peered inside.

"How should we *bloody know?"* Margo answered.

They'd agreed to remove their jewellery in case Darcy described it to the police later. Nora had gauged they must be close to the two-minute mark by now, but then she dithered, unsure.

"Fuck it. We're going in." She went first, creeping inside and leading the way.

In the foyer, Lucia whispered, "Bugger, I forgot to get Barry's hammer out of the car."

"For fuck's sake," Nora whispered back and ran to the front door. She snatched up a large umbrella from the stand and took it back to Lucia.

"You expect me to use that *as a weapon?" Lucia hissed.*

"It's better than nothing."

Margo giggled again, fuck it.

They took a left into the sitting room and fanned out. Edie waited beside the sofa on the left, a kitchen knife in hand; Margo stood opposite her, hiding next to a tall display unit, holding a tyre iron; Lucia remained to the left of the door with the umbrella. It had a long, pointed steel end that could hurt if she jabbed it hard enough. Nora went to Quenton at the back where he stood by the fireplace. She moved behind him and took the gun out of her pocket, pressing the business end to his temple. Just holding it was enough to get her shaking.

The plan:

Quenton shouting for Darcy's help to get her down here.

Darcy going to the corner for Edie, Lucia, and Margo to guard her.

Nora marching Quenton into the drawing room to get the jewels from the safe.

Nora ordering him to tie Darcy up with rope he'd hidden prior to their arrival.

Nora tying Quenton up.

The getaway.

Quenton making a show of trying to get his ropes off, allowing enough time to pass for them to reach Nora's house before he phoned for help.

"Give the word when you want this to begin," she said quietly.

"The boys, they're not asleep yet—it's still light out, so they think it's not time for bed."

"Then why didn't you tell us to come later when it's dark if you knew they fucked about if Patty wasn't the one sorting them out?"

Edie gave him a scathing look.

"Just do it now," Quenton ordered. "If the lads come down, they come down."

"If they come down," Nora said, "that's more people to worry about—they could phone the police! We **talked** *about this!"*

They all paused at the sound of clip-clopping on the marble foyer floor. Everyone stared at the doorway, Lucia brandishing the umbrella. Darcy appeared, one foot in the sitting room, the other in the foyer. Her lovely hair, usually in her signature chignon, lay on her shoulders in golden waves. Her silk dressing gown and matching pyjamas, a lush dark purple, matched her dainty slippers.

"Oh God," she whispered.

"Come in here slowly or I'll blow his head off," Nora said, roughing up her East End accent. "Don't do anything stupid."

Darcy glanced to her right—the telephone was that way on top of an occasional table. She must have thought better of it and gave Nora her attention. What had just gone through her mind? Did she worry that if Quenton died, she'd be turfed out of Goosemoor by Senior and wouldn't be a lady anymore? Or was she worried about her children?

She took one step forward. Two. Then caught sight of Lucia and the umbrella. She reached out to snatch it.

Nora panicked and aimed the gun at the floor. She fired.

Darcy shrieked, her hand dropping to her side. "Please, I—"

"Don't fuck us about, got it?" Nora snarled.

Margo stepped out from the side of the display unit and slapped the tyre iron against her gloved palm. Edie pointed the knife Darcy's way. Lucia lunged forward and jabbed the umbrella point into the woman's arm.

"Do what they say," Quenton said.

Darcy stared over at him. "How did they even get in?"

"The staff door was left unlocked."

Darcy blinked. "Patty...that's Patty's job."

Quenton cleared his throat. "She must have forgotten to do it before she left."

Darcy glared at Nora. "Did Patty arrange this? Did she send you here?"

"Mummy?"

Oh, for fuck's sake…

One of the boys appeared next to Darcy, then the other, a bit too close to the poking-out umbrella. Quenton groaned. Margo sucked in a quick breath.

Edie whipped the knife out of sight. Darcy grasped their hands but didn't retreat.

What kind of mother didn't tell their kids to run to safety?

Nora raised the gun. "Go and stand in the corner with the children." She jerked the gun to indicate she meant the corner behind Lucia.

Darcy didn't move.

"Didn't you fucking hear me?" Nora shrieked.

Darcy narrowed her eyes. "Nora?"

"Who?" Nora could kick herself for speaking in her normal voice. "I don't know a fucking Nora."

"It is you…"

"Don't be ridiculous," Quenton said. "Nora's a loyal member of staff, she wouldn't do something like this."

"It's her." Darcy made eye contact. "Get out, you stupid girl."

Girl? Who the hell does she think she's talking to?

Nora stalked forward until she was halfway across the room.

"Why are you just standing there, Quenton?" Darcy shouted. "Hit her with the poker!"

The boys trembled, and one cried.

"Just do as she asks," Quenton begged her. "Go into the corner."

"No." Darcy stood her ground. "Absolutely not."

"Shoot her before we all end up in prison," Quenton commanded in a sharp whisper.

Before Nora could think about what she was doing, she aimed and pulled the trigger. The bullet hit Darcy in the chest, and she went down, her sons still holding her hands and going to the floor with her. They screamed, all three of them, as well as Edie and Margo. Lucia just stared at them, then at Nora, her mouth open, and Quenton moved forward to stand beside Nora.

"Shit," she said. "Shit!"

"Mummy!" one boy wailed. "Wake up!"

The other got up and rushed for the doorway.

"Shoot him!" Quenton hissed.

Nora fired again—God fucking forgive her, but panic had taken a firm hold. Voices erupted all at once: Quenton quietly saying to finish the other boy, too, that it would be kinder; Margo shouting, "He's just a kid, Nora, a fucking kid!"; Lucia barking that they had to get out of there; and Edie, waffling on about calling an ambulance.

Nora shot the other son.

What have I done?

Her friends converged on her, Edie grabbing her arm ready to propel her from the room, all of them babbling. It was too much. The noise. The guilt. All of it. Nora had worked for Quenton for years, and when he told her to do something, she jumped to it. She'd been conditioned and had automatically obeyed, even though his order had been to kill.

How the hell had that happened?

"Quiet!" Quenton roared. "For goodness sake, shut up, every bloody one of you!"

The room silenced. Nora took in the carnage. She'd killed a mother and her children. The panic and Quenton had been too difficult to ignore, a trio of knee-jerk reactions: if those three had lived, they would have been witnesses.

"Did you bring a bag?" Quenton asked as if his family hadn't been slain.

"Fuck, I forgot it," Lucia said.

"Like you forgot the hammer?" Margo seethed. "Hurry up. I need to get the hell out of here. I think I'm going to be sick."

Quenton led the charge into the drawing room, everyone stepping over the bodies. He unlocked the safe hidden behind a framed painting. Lucia opened the umbrella to halfway, creating a bag of sorts, and Quenton dropped the jewellery cases inside.

"Wait," Margo said. "I want to see what's inside those. You could be stiffing us. For all we know, this wasn't meant to be about money at all but murder." She poked a shaking finger towards Quenton. "I heard what you said to Nora. You gave her the green light to shoot that gun."

Quenton removed the cases and opened each one, revealing that there were, indeed, jewels inside. He closed them, put them back in the umbrella. Then he took out the remaining ones from the safe, revealed their contents, too, and added them to the haul. Lucia shut the umbrella as best she could and bunched it at the top.

"These had better be the real deal and not that paste shit," Margo said.

Nora hadn't thought of that possibility, Quenton having fakes made up. What if he had? Then this had been about murdering Darcy and the kids after all?

Fuck.

"Of course they are," Quention said. "You can't take the umbrella with you, Patty will know it's gone. She keeps an inventory."

"We'll empty it in the car." Margo gave Quenton one last filthy look and left the room.

"See you tomorrow, Nora," Quenton said.

Nora nodded. She followed Margo out to the car, shaken over what she'd done, Edie and Lucia behind her. They had twenty minutes to get home before Quenton phoned the police, so they had to hurry. Nora clicked the safety on and stuffed the gun back in her pocket. Lucia and Margo had already emptied the umbrella, and Lucia passed it to Nora who handed it off to Edie. Edie gave it to Quenton on the threshold.

He closed the door.

Silent, they got in the car. Nora drove away, keeping tears at bay.

"You're a bitch," Margo said to her.

"I panicked."

"Kids, Nora…"

"I know."

"That's going to haunt me for the rest of my life."

No one said anything else. There was no need. It would haunt all of them.

Chapter Twelve

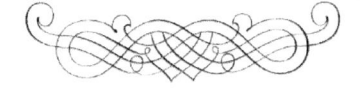

In one of his less expensive cars so as not to draw attention to himself, Ulysses drove towards the manor, something he'd gone past before but had never entered. He hadn't been invited to any parties; Quenton had worried that their affection for one another would shine through, Darcy and the staff seeing it. There hadn't *been* any affection on Ulysses' part, or maybe he should correct himself and say Vincent, someone he'd stopped being the minute he'd hit the big time. It helped to see himself as two different people—the one before and the one after.

Vincent had always wanted to be famous, and he'd done everything necessary to achieve that. He'd used Quenton for a place to live, secretly entertaining showbiz men in the townhouse, having sex with them in the hope they'd cast him in their films or plays, or praying those who were already actors passed his name to someone higher up the chain. He'd lost count of the blow jobs he'd given.

The love letters Vincent had written, all lies, all designed to convince Quenton to keep him at the house as his dirty little secret. Vincent had acted so well, so how could he *not* be destined for fame? But he'd needed somewhere to live of his own. Bribing Quenton had come about one night when Vincent had drunk too much, his mind seeming to conjure the plan all by itself.

It had gone without a hitch. For Vincent. For Quenton, not so much, as those robbers had killed his horsey-looking wife and those two brats of hers. Vincent had wondered whether Quenton had arranged for that to happen, so he'd asked him outright. Quenton had denied it, his reply so vehement Vincent believed him.

Or was Quenton an actor, too? He must have been in order to hide everything from his wife, his parents, and the staff for so long.

Ulysses swerved onto the driveway and gunned it towards the manor, his dream of actually living there going up in smoke the moment Quenton had mentioned keeping the letters. But he could get things back on the right track. He'd passed him the business card so they could reconnect, him acting once again to pretend he still loved him, that his mistake from the past had dogged him ever since. Now all he had to do was persuade Quenton to destroy the evidence, Ulysses would move into the manor—or the Gables would be nicer—and do whatever he could to ensure the man died of a heart attack and left all of his worldly goods to him.

His current ex-lover, a spiteful bitch of a younger man, would likely cause trouble once it appeared in the news that Ulysses was now with a lord. Those bloody journalists with their lying rags were the bane of his life at times but a godsend in others. Life as an older actor was about as close to perfect as it could get—until Quenton had dropped his bombshell. Still, it wouldn't take much to reel him back in.

Ulysses parked in front of the building and paused for a moment to take in the grandeur displayed in the beams from the bright headlights. There had to be at least twenty bedrooms. He could host lavish parties here, his friends staying over, and he'd be the talk of the town. His current place, a modern effort with too many huge windows instead of walls, was a beauty, but nothing spoke of wealth and elegance like a stately home.

He got out of the car and walked to the front door, tugging a rope he assumed rang the bell. It chimed loudly then echoed. Oh, that foyer must be huge. Excited to finally get to see inside, to view the curio cabinet Quenton had spoken about far too many times, its contents apparently worth a fortune, Ulysses totted up how much he'd get for selling the place. With no heirs for Quenton to pass Goosemoor and the Gables to, Ulysses would be quids in.

Provided he could convince him they belonged together.

The door opened, and Ulysses hid his shock at how haggard Quenton appeared this evening compared to at the charity ball. Had Ulysses' admission affected him *that* much? Ulysses' suit was a far superior outfit compared to the bobbled cardigan and tweed trousers Quenton had on, and that shirt…bloody awful. Was that a stain on it? Had he fallen on hard times? Didn't the money from those posh people who rented the Gables cover his expenses?

Ulysses cleared his throat. "Good evening."

"Not for you. Come in."

What did he mean by that?

Ulysses stepped inside, and he'd been right, the foyer *was* huge. "Are you going to show off the contents of your cabinet to me? I recall you telling me you used to enjoy bragging about that to visitors."

Ulysses glanced over there. Only a few items remained on the shelves, yet Quenton had told him it had contained numerous things. Had he been selling them one by one over the years? Was Ulysses' assessment correct and Quenton was low on money? A gold stag stood proud on the top shelf. If that was real gold, it would fetch a damn good price.

Quenton closed the door. "Small talk isn't necessary. We both know why you're here, so we'll just get down to business, shall we?"

Ulysses smiled despite anger flaring. What he'd seen so far didn't bode well at all. He'd thought Quenton would be loaded, but maybe he wasn't. Still, the two properties alone would generate a nice pay packet.

He followed him into a drawing room. It matched his imagination from when Quenton had described it to him years ago, apart from different wallpaper.

Quenton patted him down, avoiding eye contact. Didn't he believe Ulysses wouldn't bring his phone? He'd contemplated ignoring that order and leaving it in the car, but getting Quenton to trust him was paramount, so he'd obeyed. He'd told his staff he was going to bed early and had dismissed them.

No one knew he was here.

"Sit." Quenton pointed to an unsightly yellow chaise longue and sat in a green wingback chair. "I hate you, but manners prevail. Do you want a drink? Whiskey?"

"I'm driving. Unless I can stay overnight." Ulysses winked and smirked.

"Err, no. I can see what you're doing, trying to give me all that charm of yours, but it won't work. I'm only interested in getting back what's mine. Forty-five thousand pounds."

Ulysses sat, a laugh erupting. Was this man for real? And it was even *more* obvious now that he was running low on funds. "But I only asked you for five."

"Inflation." Quenton lit a cigarette.

Ulysses supposed it was only right. It wasn't as if he couldn't afford to pay it. "Okay, that's fine."

Quenton huffed. "Look how *easy* it is for you. You can pay me and not bat an eyelid. You don't have to set up a damn robbery."

"That was…unfortunate. You never told me you were short on cash, you always looked so nice in those expensive suits. I assumed—"

"—wrong, that's what you assumed." Quenton grunted. "Things aren't always as they seem. You knew *exactly* what I had to do to get that money because I told you afterwards. Didn't you feel even the slightest bit guilty?"

"Of course I did," Ulysses lied. "Like I told you at the ball, I've hated myself ever since. It was a horrible, horrible thing to do. I was young and selfish. You have no idea how much I've regretted what I did."

"You didn't regret it enough to come here and pay me back once you'd made your millions, though, did you? No, you partied your life away, soaked in the adoration, made people think you're a benevolent, kind man by giving to charity, but underneath it all you're just scum. Thieving scum."

This wasn't going as Ulysses had expected. How *stupid* he'd been to think that time wouldn't have changed the man. He'd foolishly remembered Quenton as he was the last time he'd seen him before the ball—desperate, pleading, begging for one more chance. He'd altered beyond recognition.

Ulysses tried another tactic. "If you give me your bank details, I'll see to the transfer once I get home. You said not to bring my phone with me, so I can't access the app…"

"You can use my laptop. Sign in to your bank from there." Quenton pulled an older-model machine from down by the side of his chair and opened it. "Here, log in."

Ulysses got up and took the laptop back to the chaise. He Googled for his bank's website and put in his details and the passcode. "I can see you don't believe how sorry I am, how I thought—"

"*What* did you think?"

"That we could try again. I could make amends. I...no one else has made me feel like you did. I didn't realise what we had. I want to make it up to you."

Quenton laughed. Smoked as if Ulysses wasn't even there. Then he barked, "Get on with it then!" He recited a sort code and account number from a notebook.

Ulysses typed them in. "It's asking for the name on the account."

"Brothers Investments."

"A business of yours?"

"That's not your concern."

Ulysses had set it so he could send up to one hundred thousand in a single transaction—he loved to purchase high-end things—but if the bank flagged it, stopped it from going through...

It didn't. The money disappeared from his previous total, barely making a dent. Forty-five thousand to him was like forty-five pounds.

"No one can say I don't repay my debts now," he said, logging out and putting the laptop to one side.

Quenton got up and collected the laptop and, using a cloth from his side table, wiped it all over.

Why's he doing that? To get rid of my fingerprints? What for?

Regardless of the unease creeping through him, Ulysses would have to try again. The sale of Quenton's houses was too important to give up now. "I really am sorry."

"I don't believe you. Now get out. And *don't* come back."

Ulysses rose, not yet admitting defeat. Quenton would come round eventually. "Please, I'll show you I'm different. I was desperate back then, a silly little boy, greedy for money and fame. I've matured now…"

"I don't care. Piss off."

Ulysses couldn't leave yet. He'd clout Quenton if he had to, then search the place. "What about the letters?"

"What about them?"

"Can you at least burn them in front of me? I've paid what you wanted, so there's no need to get the police involved or out me in the press."

"What you did meant Darcy and the boys died. I think you need to pay for that."

"Pardon?"

"You heard him."

Ulysses spun round at the sound of another voice, his heart skipping several beats, his chest seeming to hollow out. Two bearded men in forensic suits stared at him from the doorway. What the hell? Police? Had Quenton called them already? Was their conversation a way to get Ulysses to confess?

"You're coming with us," one of them said. "We were going to take you off for a little chat, but you've spewed what happened already, so there's no need."

"Are you…are you *arresting* me?"

The man smiled. "Nah, I'm killing you."

Chapter Thirteen

Quenton hated being told what to do, so having a blindfold put on, his wrists cuffed behind his back so he couldn't take it off, and being marched out of his own home like *he* was the criminal, it annoyed him immensely. It wasn't as if he could do or say anything about it either, not when the thugs were in charge. The vehicle he'd been placed in—it could be a van as he *certainly* hadn't been put onto a seat—had come to a stop, so he assumed they were at traffic lights or they'd reached their destination. Quenton understood why he wasn't allowed to see the route, but really!

"Please," Ulysses whispered, the word creepy and sudden. "Please put a stop to this, Quenny."

"Why the devil *should* I?" Quenton barked. "You brought this all on yourself. And don't call me that. You don't have the right anymore."

A deep chuckle—it had to be George or Greg—then the van moved off again.

"They're going to kill me," Ulysses whined.

"I know, I heard what George said."

"You said you're going to watch," Ulysses muttered.

"They offered, and I accepted. I want to make sure you're really dead. The amount of suffering I went through because of you…"

"Are you talking about Darcy and the boys? Because you told me you didn't even love them."

"I had a marriage of convenience, you know damn well I did, so if you're trying to make me feel bad, don't bother. Besides, I wasn't talking about her *or* the children."

"What then?"

Quenton wasn't sure he wanted to reveal the raw emotions that had bitten chunks out of him for months, years. "I took our breakup badly, that's all I'm telling you."

"So you *did* love me. I had no idea how much…"

"What, did you think I was *lying*?" Quenton hissed. "You *know* I jolly well loved you. I wouldn't have taken the risk and set you up in the townhouse if I didn't. What, are you going to now say if you'd known the depths of it, you'd never have sent me those letters? No, you would have, because greed is your middle name."

The van bumped and jostled, sending Quenton sliding across the floor so he found himself wedged against Ulysses. He scrabbled away, desperate to put space between them. The contact sent a shudder through him.

The van stopped. He imagined George and Greg got out, then came the sound of the back door opening. Quenton waited to be guided to wherever, hating that he had to rely on others to help him. Someone gripped his upper arms and hefted him out, depositing him on what felt like grass, the ground springy beneath his slippers—

the big men hadn't even waited for him to change into his shoes, for God's sake! One hand let go of one arm, and he was led along by the other, his feet now on what he imagined was concrete—a path?—then an inside floor. He walked on, the creak of a door opening, and he was pushed down onto a seat.

"The cuffs and blindfold can come off shortly," George said.

The noises of more movement. George must have walked away, but extra footsteps merged with his, and Quenton presumed Greg and Ulysses had joined him. A door closed, the blindfold removed. Quenton blinked beneath the stark light, assessing his surroundings. A steel-lined room? And oh, goodness, chains hung from the ceiling, and what he guessed was a trapdoor had been set in the floor.

Ulysses stood between George and Greg who started stripping his clothes off. Ulysses struggled against them, but it was pointless. Every time he tried to sidestep them, the twins moved into his path. By the time he had nothing on, he was a sweating mess, his face red from either embarrassment or anger. He covered his private parts with both hands. Quenton revelled in the bastard's discomfort. He deserved every bit of this humiliation, hunched over, naked and vulnerable.

Between them, The Brothers snapped manacles attached to the chains on Ulysses' wrists. George wound a handle on the wall. Ulysses rose until he hung around a foot off the floor. He reached with his toes to find purchase, but the tips were just shy of the steel. He swung to and fro, Quenton, George, and Greg staring at him.

Eventually, Ulysses became still, his eyes brimming. "Please, I don't want to die…"

"Not many people do, sunshine," George said, "but in your case, tough. You took that choice away from yourself the second you sent Quenton those letters. Karma took her sweet time, but she's here now."

Quenton remembered the night someone had come to collect the envelope from under the mat outside the front door. All day, he'd worried Patty would send someone to scrub the step, despite him telling her that job was off the roster that day, his excuse that it was raining, so what was the point? Quenton and Darcy had been in the drawing room that evening, Patty not long departing for home after putting the boys to bed. The crunch of shoes or boots on the gravel driveway had sent Quenton to the window.

"Is that Patty coming back?" Darcy asked absently, her nose in a book.

Quenton stared at the shape of a person. "Nobody's out there, dear."

"But I heard them."

"I thought I did, too, but we must have been mistaken."

The person had approached the front door, the outside light shining on them. All in black clothing, a balaclava hiding their face, they were slim, wiry, and seemed young as they employed stealth to snatch Quenton's reply letter from beneath the mat then sprint off into the darkness, over the grass, heading towards the tree line bordering the main road.

"Ah, a fox," Quenton said.

"Bloody things." Darcy yawned. "I think I'll go to bed."

They didn't share a room, hadn't since the third time he couldn't 'perform', and he was glad. He could stare at the ceiling in his own room, worrying about what would happen next with Mr Orchid. Would another letter arrive at the office again, or even worse, here?

He'd be living on his nerves until he found out.

Quenton remembered how he'd felt waiting for it to appear. "Like I said in the van, I hate you for what you did to me. Not just because I loved you, but because you were so cruel in that second letter. There was no need for that. And to think you came to Goosemoor tonight, asking for us to try again. You're evil. Did you not realise you were also talking about yourself with what you wrote? Or was that so I wouldn't think it was you? Do you have any idea how ashamed you made me feel?"

Dear Lord Goosemoor,

You are a disgusting man. God will smite you for fornicating with another of the same sex. It isn't allowed, and if you were truly a Christian, you'd heed the teachings. You deserve to have your penis chopped off so you can never sin again.

*Do you fancy those little boys, too? Do you wish you could touch **them**?*

You deviant! Filth!

Leave the money in a paper bag in the men's toilets of the Fiddle and Bow in Dormand Street,

tomorrow night, 8 p.m. Try not to fondle anyone while you're in there, won't you?
　Regards,
　Mr Orchid

Quenton repeated the gist of the letter to the twins.

Ulysses shook his head. "It was...it was directed at myself. *I* was ashamed. What we did, what I did with others, I'd been taught it was wrong but couldn't help myself. It wasn't until years later that I was all right with who I am."

"So you decided to take your shame out on *me*?" Quenton roared. "You bastard! I did nothing but treat you nicely. And even after I paid you that money, you used me. For the holidays, the parties, all of it. Then you dumped me as if I didn't matter at all. You became Ulysses King—and it's fitting that you chose that name, because you really are King Wrathful."

George frowned. "What the chuff are you on about?"

"Ulysses means wrathful, full of anger—which he was at times," Quenton explained.

George harrumphed. "How the fuck do you know *that*?"

"I looked it up many years ago in the library." Quenton had been obsessed with the man even after their split, wanting to remain tethered to him, if only by leafing through an encyclopaedia or seeing him on the cinema screen.

"I didn't mean any of it," Ulysses said. "I swear I didn't."

Quenton glared at him. "You meant every word, and they were directed at *me*, not you. You'll say anything to be let go."

"I've had enough of this bollocks," George said. "It's not getting us anywhere or solving anything."

He moved over to a table in the corner and picked up a mace, the handle long with a spike-covered ball on top. It had a slim chain on the end of the handle and a loop on the end of that, similar to a dog's lead.

"I'd go and stand by the door if I were you," Greg said.

Quenton assumed it was so he didn't get hurt. He followed him over there. Greg undid the handcuffs then passed him some gloves and a white suit from a nearby box on the floor. Quenton got dressed over his clothes, watching George. The man was a maniac. He held the leather loop and swung the mace in a circle at his side, narrowly missing Ulysses every time.

"I beg you, don't do this," Ulysses said.

"You can beg all you like, my old son, but it won't make a blind bit of difference to me. You'll get what you deserve. Who the fuck do you think you are trying to make him feel bad about his sexuality? Fucking arsewipe."

"I—"

"Shut up, I'm not buying any excuses. You knew it'd play on his mind. As for implying he's a kiddie fiddler... You're sick in the head, you are." George glanced over at Quenton, the mace coming to a swinging stop. "Ready?"

Quenton nodded.

"If you need to barf, there's a bathroom out there."

"Barf?"

"Be sick."

George smiled, repositioned himself, then swung the mace in a circle again. He eased closer and closer to Ulysses who brought his knees up, obviously worried his tackle would get scratched. The mace bit into his chest first, embedding so the spikes in the flesh were no longer visible. Ulysses screamed, and George tugged on the chain, the mace breaking free, skin ripping. George repeated his actions again and again. Blood, so much blood, more screams, Ulysses sobbing. The weapon caught his face, two spikes digging into his bottom lip. George yanked it, the lip tearing downwards, revealing teeth and gums and blood. Ulysses' screeching was music to Quenton's ears, and each time the mini spears found a new spot, the screeches grew louder.

George attacked him for a long time, no part of the body left unscathed. Blood covered the trapdoor in spatters. George dropped the mace on the floor and went over to a hose wound around a holder on the wall. He unravelled some and turned a tap on. He blasted Ulysses, the water on so forcefully that some of the holes opened, little thirsty mouths. He washed the body then aimed the water at the ruined face, Ulysses whimpering and sobbing and gasping.

It was then Quenton spotted something. He bent over and laughed at what should be awful but was bloody brilliant. Ulysses, reduced to a bleeding mess, the end of his prized possession on the floor, the rest of his cock and balls mangled, a testicle half hanging out of the sac. Quenton stood upright, fascinated by more blood pouring from the once-clean wounds. George shut the tap off and collected a sword from the table.

Quention took it from George and plunged it into Ulysses' stomach. There, he'd transferred all of his pain to him. He pulled the sword back out, reversed a few steps. Then he ran at him, rammed it in again, shoving forward with all his weight, pushing Ulysses backwards on the chains. The sword's tip protruded from his back. Quenton sidestepped then let the handle go. Ulysses swung backwards and forwards, blood spewing from his mouth in a sputtering eruption.

Quention shouted above Ulysses' fresh screams, "I rather think a cup of tea is in order, don't you?" He'd had enough. He took the forensic clothing off and left it on the floor.

An hour later, George came into the kitchen and announced he'd got rid of the body. Quenton frowned—he hadn't heard the van's engine—but did he really care where Ulysses had gone? No. But if he changed his mind about that he could imagine it. An earthy grave, or perhaps a watery one. Either way, the twins had promised Ulysses would never be found.

"The fucker wouldn't die, so I had to finish him off," George said. "I slit his throat." He sat and took a cup of coffee from his brother. "The room's nice and clean, and the suits and gloves have been bagged up ready for the fire."

Greg nodded and gestured to Quenton. "We'll nip you back to the manor in a bit, then."

Quenton thanked him. "I appreciate what you've done."

"Sorry you had to go through all that with him back then—you know, him making you feel bad." George sipped. "Some people can be right cunts, can't they."

Quenton agreed, although with those orders he'd given Nora on the night of the robbery, he might just be the biggest one.

Chapter Fourteen

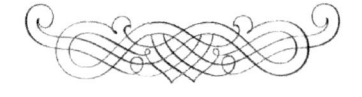

Nora drove towards the manor the next morning full of trepidation and fear, the rawness of her emotions exacerbated by her lack of sleep. Her nerves, brittle and waiting to snap, seemed to buzz inside her. She was knackered, had no choice but to keep going — she had to get through the next part of the plan

whether she liked it or not. If she didn't arrive at work this morning it would look odd.

She gasped and checked the rearview, convinced she'd seen something flicker in the mirror. The ghostly shadows of the three dead people seemed to sit in the car with her, and a shiver wended up her spine, goosebumps sprinting all over her.

She turned onto the driveway, that fear ramping up.

An officer in uniform held his hand up to stop her. She rolled down her window, shitting bricks. Was he going to turn her away? Or was he going to ask her where she'd been last night?

"Name, please?" Brusque. Official.

Nora frowned at him—what would a normal, innocent person say? "What's happened?"

"Name."

Bloody hell, jobsworth! "Nora Robbins."

He checked something in his notebook and gave her the nod. Quenton said he'd put her on an approved list, but it still seemed strange that she could go to work as if nothing was wrong. Was the investigation in the house almost at an end if she was allowed up there? She supposed it might be if they'd been there all night.

She proceeded along the driveway, nauseated. A police car and van out the front wasn't a shock, but the sight of them still sent her stomach rolling over. The front door stood open, strangers milling in and out, just as ghostly as the unseen spirits in the back of her car. They appeared to be packing things away in the van. She drove around the back and parked between Patty's and Cook's cars. Two other maids were in, their vehicles also there. She switched the engine off and sat for a moment, catching sight of an officer's reflection in the rearview. He stood at the tradesman's entrance giving her the once-over. She ignored him, but he came over to tap on her window.

She lowered it. "Yes?"

"What are you doing just sitting there?"

"I don't start work for another five minutes so I was going to smoke a fag like usual. What's happened? Is everyone okay?"

"I'll leave it for Lord Goosemoor to have a word with you." He backed away to his post.

Nora got her baccy tin out and lit a rollie. Her nerves were shot, so she needed the nicotine. Would he think she was suspicious for being so casual, smoking?

Last night, when they'd arrived at her house, they'd all got drunk. She'd tried to explain how something inside her had taken over when Quenton had told her to kill Darcy and her boys, but her explanation of obeying him while she worked here didn't seem to hold water with her friends. So she'd moved on to another excuse: Darcy had recognised her voice, and had she lived, she'd have told the coppers. Margo had suggested she could have put on a man's voice and threatened Darcy with harm so she didn't grass Nora up.

"Why didn't you do that at the time, then?" Nora had blasted back at her. "Why didn't you do it before I pulled the trigger? You heard him tell me what to do, and you didn't stop it."

"You said we had to stick to his fucking plan, that's why!"

Quenton chirping in her ear had resulted in Nora reacting, and she'd stick by that. But she shouldn't have done it three times. Those children hadn't deserved to die, but self-preservation had been so strong inside her she hadn't thought about anything else. It was no excuse, she should have had more control over her actions, but she hadn't, and now she was a killer. She'd already been one by proxy, what with Ron arranging for Oscar to be murdered, but that didn't seem so bad. Oscar had earned his death, the others hadn't.

Margo had cried on and off, and it was understandable why. She had kids of her own—her mother had looked after them overnight—and she couldn't get her head around why Quenton had given Nora the go-ahead to shoot his sons. Lucia and Edie had piped up with much the same, and Nora had to agree it was bloody weird, evil. Quenton had never paid his lads any mind, it was something the staff commented on regularly, how emotionally distant he was, but if she wasn't mistaken, he'd actually wanted *them dead for more than being witnesses to a robbery.*

He had to be rotten to his core.

I'm not much better.

Eleven o'clock had rolled round, and a taxi had arrived at Nora's, whisking her friends away. Being alone in her house had given her the opportunity to sift through her feelings, which she hadn't dallied over for long. One, they were too invasive, and two, she had more pressing things to think about other than little boys dying—wicked but true.

It had been light out, so her car was fully visible on the way back. Yes, they'd removed their balaclavas as soon as they'd hit the road outside the manor, burning them in her fireplace when they'd got in, but would someone recall seeing them in that area once the robbery appeared on the news? Had a neighbour heard and seen their return? Would Roger ask where her car was for part of the evening as it hadn't been around the front? She'd waited until three a.m. to put it back in its usual place, anxious in case the sound of the engine brought him to his bedroom window, insomniac that he was. When he saw it this morning, would that prompt him to question her?

Then there was the visit to Essex to see Pinocchio later today. Quenton would send her home early, an orchestrated move so she could sell the jewellery before the weekend. Then she had to get back, meet him to hand over his portion of the cash, hide the rest at home until it could be distributed between her and the others. She'd buy a safe and get someone to install it in the wall above her fireplace at some point in the future—the ruby set would go in there, her insurance against Quenton. She'd already been to her cleaning job at the pub this morning, not bothering to go to bed as she started at five. Her mind was clogged and fuzzy—what if she fucked up once she went inside the manor? The police would want to speak to her, surely.

She stubbed her rollie out in the ashtray, got out of the car, and gave her name to the officer on guard. He checked his notebook, too, deemed her okay to go inside, and she walked past him into the corridor. Stopped and took a deep breath. On she went, into the foyer, sunlight streaming in through the open front door to paint the floor in a bright rectangle. Dust motes floated in the shaft, momentarily mesmerising her, keeping her focused on them instead of glancing to her left at the sitting room doorway.

She wasn't ready to do that yet.

Someone calling her name snapped her back to the horrific present.

Quenton and a man in a grey suit came towards her from the direction of the office on the right.

Dread sluiced through her body. "What's happened, sir? Why are the police here?"

"Come into my office," Quenton said. "Detective Lint would like to speak to you."

"Me? Why?"

Lint held out a hand for Nora to shake. "Just a few questions."

She shook it, his palm warm and sweaty around her cold fingers. She followed them into the office and waited for Quenton to tell her to sit—she had to act the same as she would in normal circumstances. He gestured to the armchair, and she sank onto it, thankful as her legs had gone wobbly. Quenton sat behind his desk, and Lint perched his bum on the corner of it.

"What's going on?" Nora asked.

Lint, who reminded her of a bulldog chewing a wasp, speared her with an alarming, scary gaze, his eyes an unusual light shade of blue. "Where were you yesterday evening between eight and ten?"

"What? At home."

"Can anyone verify that? A husband, perhaps?"

She hung her head. "My husband's dead."

"Ah, I'm sorry. Also, I forgot to ask your name, so I apologise again. It's been a long night."

Hasn't it just. "Nora Robbins."

"Oh. Are you…?"

She looked up at him. "Yes, the wife of the man murdered in The Eagle."

"How are you bearing up? It must still be so raw. It happened so recently."

She gestured around the room. "I've got no choice but get on with things, keep coming to work. I'm the only one bringing in a wage now."

"I understand. So, last night…could those men have come here for you? Did they make a mistake in thinking you'd be at work?"

"So you're saying they might be to do with the man who shot my husband?"

"I have to cover all bases. Is there any reason, that you know of, why someone would be after you **and** your husband?"

"I haven't upset anyone, and I don't think he did either."

"Okay, back to last night."

"I had friends round. They got to mine about seven and stayed until eleven."

"Could I have their names, please?" Lint took a notepad out.

Nora recited them, plus gave their addresses. "The neighbours…they've been bringing meals round, you know, to help me out, and the fridge was full, so we had dinner together. I can't manage all that food by myself, and I don't have a freezer other than a little ice box in the fridge so it would have gone off." She was waffling but couldn't stop herself. "Oscar would have liked the stews, but he's not here to eat them and…"

She wailed, eyes scrunched shut, hoping she appeared as a grieving widow. A hand patted her shoulder. Nora composed herself and glanced up. Lint stood there, peering down, his expression one of sadness.

"My wife passed away, so I get it." He crouched, too close. "I know you've been through a distressing ordeal losing your husband, but I have some more news you'll likely find upsetting."

Nora glanced from him to Quenton. "What…? Are you okay, sir?"

"I'm bearing up, thank you for asking."

Nora studied Lint for suspicion in his eyes, but there wasn't any.

He sighed. "There was a robbery here last night. They took all of Lady Goosemoor's jewellery."

"Oh my God!" She slapped a hand to her mouth then took it away to pinch her chin. "But how did they find the safe? It's behind a picture. No one would know that unless they worked here. How did they get it open?"

"Lord Goosemoor was forced to reveal where it was at gunpoint. Four men, each with weapons. Have you heard any talk amongst the staff about planning a robbery? The housekeeper maybe?"

"What? No! Everyone here is too nice for that, and the only man is Chevvy, the gardener, and he's too old."

"Okay. Sadly, Lady Goosemoor and the children lost their lives."

Nora couldn't look at Quenton—the hatred she harboured for him would show on her face. "I can't…oh, those poor little boys… I'm so sorry, sir."

"Thank you." Quenton sounded suitably upset.

She fixed her attention on Lint. "How? I mean…"

"They were shot," Lint said bluntly. "That's why I wondered if it was linked to your husband's death."

A tap at the door drew her gaze to it, saving her from having to answer. She had no idea what she would have said.

Lint stood and called, "Yes?"

The door opened, and a police officer popped his head inside. "Removal is about to take place, sir."

Lint nodded then stared at Quenton. "Best to stay in here for the time being. It can be distressing, seeing your loved ones being taken away. Give us a few minutes."

Quenton put his elbows on the desk and propped his face in his hands, the sounds of sobbing filling the room. All an act, Nora would bet. Lint left, closing the door, and she glared over at her boss.

He spread two fingers apart and peeped through the gap, a beady eye showing, then lowered this hands to the desk and swung his gaze to her. No tears on his cheeks. He smirked. "He doesn't suspect a thing. You did brilliantly."

"Brilliantly?" she whisper-shouted. "I was up all sodding night. I killed your wife and kids, for fuck's sake—on your orders. What the hell did you do that for? The life insurance?"

"Don't be ridiculous. And you could have ignored me," he whispered back.

Oh, so he was going to put the blame on her, was he? "Yes, I could, but I was in a right state by that point. I didn't know what to do. When Darcy recognised my voice, I shit myself."

"It's done, we can't change it, so now we move forward with the plan."

He was so unfeeling, didn't care one bit that his family had been wiped out or that Nora and the others had to live with what had happened. And that was another thing. She trusted her friends, but what if the nightmares and guilt became too overwhelming that they walked into a police station and grassed Nora up? They'd be implicating themselves as well, but sometimes doing the right thing outweighed everything else.

She needed to speak to them when she dished out the money, ensure they knew that no matter how hard it got, they had *to keep their gobs shut.*

All this because Oscar hadn't paid the fucking rent!

She sat in silence for a while, then asked, "How is Patty this morning?"

"Understandably upset. She loved the boys like they were her own."

"At least someone *did."*

"What do you mean?"

"Well, Darcy wasn't the best mother, and you're not exactly cut up about it, are you?" She thought he was vile for ordering her to shoot them, but she was even viler for doing it.

"How I feel about them is none of your concern."

"And Darcy? Why would you want her and the kids killed? So you can pretend to mourn for a while then bring your lover into the fold?"

"No. We had to save ourselves, all of us."

Nora shook her head. "You're disgusting."

"Maybe so, but it wasn't me who pulled the trigger." That smirk again.

She launched out of the chair, ready to go over there and slap his twisted face, but someone tapped on the door again, then Lint came in. Shit, had he been listening? Were they about to be arrested?

"The pathologist will be in touch, Lord Goosemoor."

Quenton stood. "Thank you."

"You're free to have the room cleaned now. We're finished here. We'll see ourselves out." He smiled at Nora. "I phoned your friends, and your alibi checks out. Again, my condolences regarding your husband. It does get easier, I promise." He left.

She flumped down onto the chair in relief. Nora and Quenton stayed there for what seemed like ages, then he strode out into the foyer. Nora got up and followed, finding him at the sitting room doorway talking to Patty who whittled her fingers, her eyes red and sore-looking. Quenton went upstairs, and Patty came closer to Nora.

"I should never have gone early last night," the housekeeper said. "But Mr Goosemoor insisted I needed some time off, and Darcy wanted to put the boys to bed, so I went. I left them, all because I was tired. If I'd been here, they would have been asleep — we had a strict routine. They wouldn't have witnessed their mother being killed. Lord Goosemoor told me what happened, and it's just dreadful."

Had she told the police he'd insisted she leave early? Wouldn't that seem odd to them?

Nora sighed. "I can't imagine what they went through."

"Neither can I. They were only little. What sort of monster kills children?"

Me. I'm that monster. *"I don't know."*

Patty straightened. Sucked in a big breath. Slapped her hands together. "Right," she said on the exhale, "Mr Goosemoor wants that blood cleaned off the carpet, so put gloves on and get to it. Plenty of bicarb in the bucket of water should do it."

Nora supposed she deserve this, to scrub the blood she'd spilled, but the copper-penny smell of it churned her stomach. At last she stared at the carpet, the dark-red splashes on the door, and she heaved.

Patty bustled off, and Nora got on with the job. She couldn't get it all out of the fibres, so Patty said to leave it to dry then have another go tomorrow. Two hours after Quenton had retreated upstairs he returned, calling Patty to join him and Nora in the foyer.

"I can see this has been too distressing for Nora, so I'm sending her home, Patty." Quenton nodded curtly and wandered into his office.

Nora made her escape via the rear door. In her car, she sat for a moment, the scent of blood in her nostrils, and allowed herself a good cry. She was a horrible person and had to learn to live with what she'd done. But not yet. She had to get home and collect the jewellery, leaving the ruby set under her bed.

It was time to visit Pinocchio.

Chapter Fifteen

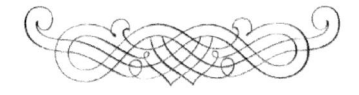

George had called a meeting in the Noodle and Tiger car park. He sat in the front of their black cab with Greg, their coppers in the back: Janine Sheldon, Bryan Flint, and Anaisha Bolton. Sometimes, messaging them wasn't enough. A face-to-face chat was needed, and five heads were better than one. They had to discuss the other abusive men and how to proceed, because no matter which way George spun it in his head, it wasn't going to work. He'd promised the women they'd get rid of their partners, and he wanted to honour that, but how? He'd already explained what had happened to Morgan, so everyone was up to date.

"What's the problem?" Flint asked. "Just off the fuckers."

Janine tutted and gave him a look that suggested she was tired of the way he didn't think outside the box, even though she'd been teaching him how to do that. "Think about it. If all their bodies turn up one after the other, the police will soon cotton on that the men are linked to women who live at Haven. If it's clear they've been murdered, it'll be me dealing with it, but there's no way even *I* can cover up that every woman lives at the refuge—Colin will be with me, remember. As a DS he's crap normally, but lately he's been taking an interest. If they're killed when I'm on maternity leave, another detective will poke into it—do we want that? Shouldn't the men be removed before then? I don't want to be bring extra work upon myself, but it does make sense."

"Yeah, I want it done while you're still able to deal with it," George said, "hence this chat: we need to find a way to do it."

Janine sighed. "Okay, Morgan's killed himself as far as anyone's concerned, so that's him covered, but even if the others are sorted later down the line, the Haven link is still going to be discovered because background checks will be done on the women as a part of the investigations."

"The same will happen if the men go 'missing' or also kill themselves," Anaisha said. "No matter how we do this, the Haven connection will always be made. Even later on when they're living in flats. Previous addresses would be checked and their lives looked into in order to get them off the suspect list."

George grunted. "My thought was that they all died at the same time in an accident. Stupid?"

Janine tapped her bottom lip with a finger. "That could work if the women say their husbands knew each other. The Haven link will still be there, but it won't look so odd. It's not unusual for a group of men to hang around together."

Anaisha shook her head. "But what *will* be odd is that all of those in the accident just happened to have beaten the women up enough that they ran away to the same place."

"We could make up a rumour after the accident," Flint said. "I can say one of my secret informants told me the blokes were in some boys' wife-beater club or something."

Greg rubbed his forehead—he appeared pained. This was obviously doing his head in, but he clearly realised the job needed to be done as soon as possible. "Would that fly, though. *Really*?"

Janine pondered that. "Think about The Network and how the members were involved in human trafficking. It happens, like-minded people forming cliques. I wouldn't be on this case because of it being an accident, so we'd just have to hope that whoever takes it on will believe Flint when he passes on what his 'informant' said."

"Maybe a day trip in a minibus," Flint suggested.

"And how are we going to get them to agree to go?" Anaisha asked. "Send them a bloody invite? Sorry, but the logistics of this are shot away.

There are too many variables. Some of the men might not want to know."

"We could set something else up," George said. "Send them emails using a VPN about winning a competition, something like that. Get them to meet somewhere at a specific time. Blow the place up or set fire to it with them inside."

"There's a row of abandoned council garages down Jacobson Street," Flint said. "It could be their meeting place, as in they went there to discuss beating women up or something."

Janine tutted. "And *that* location as a meeting place isn't going to let them know something's suss, is it. Most of the garage doors are hanging off, and homeless people are living there. Too many witnesses. Can you imagine rocking up there, seeing other men waiting, and not thinking it's strange? You'd turn around and go home again, surely."

"But something along those lines could work." George's mind ticked over. "We just need them all in one place at the same time. Where that is and the reason for them to be there can come later once we've had a think. We'll have a chat to the women, see if the blokes have anything in common—football, something like that—and the invites could be linked to that."

"What if they've got nothing in common?" Janine blew out a long breath. "I'm just saying now, for the record, that I can't *wait* to go on maternity leave. I may even use holiday up so I can take it early. This sort of shit is getting to me. I handed the reins over to Flint, so I assume, because we're talking murder, this is the reason I'm involved in this chat because it might be me who ends up running the case—if another copper realises it isn't an accident. You can't be sure what a detective might dig up." She reached over to open the door. "Unless the case gets passed to me, count me out."

"But you just suggested it gets done before maternity leave. Make your fucking mind up. Are your hormones still all over the place or what?"

She went to leave the taxi.

"Wait," George said. "There's something else I need to tell you."

Janine rolled her eyes. Gritted her teeth. *"What…"*

"Ulysses King."

"What about him?"

"He'll be reported missing at some point."

Janine slapped her knee. "Oh, wonderful. A fucking famous actor. For your sake, I hope you covered your arses *really* well on this one. What the fuck did you off *him* for? Actually, I don't want to know."

She left, slamming the door, everyone staring after her.

"That told us," George said.

Greg picked lint off his suit jacket. "Right, are we done here?"

George nodded. "Yeah, we'll speak to the women then go from there." He slapped his forehead. "It's just dawned on me. There's only one woman registered with social services as being at Haven... No one knows the others are there."

Greg gave him a filthy look. "So this meeting was for nothing because you *forgot* an important detail? For fuck's sake!"

"We've had other shit to deal with, and it only just clicked, all right? We'll fudge the tenancy agreements for the flats, make it seem like they've lived in them since before they left their fellas, no Haven in between."

Anaisha scoffed. "The block of flats you've bought recently? The police are going to clock straight away that *all* the women live there. That's just as bad a coincidence as Haven."

George wanted to scream. The obstructions were doing his nut in. "We have other flats. They belong to a shell company on paper. We can dot the women around the East End so they don't live near each other." He smiled. "Sorted."

"Apart from getting the men in the same place at the same time," Anaisha said.

"Yeah, that all hinges on what the women can tell us." George's stomach rumbled. "Okay, you two can fuck off. I need some grub."

Flint and Anaisha left the taxi, getting into their own vehicles and driving away.

George smiled at Greg. "Fancy eating in the Noodle?"

Greg nodded. "Can do."

They entered the pub via the back door.

Nessa, their manager, came out of the loos holding a mop and bucket and smiled at them. "Food?"

"You know us too well," George said.

"I'll just put this away and wash my hands."

While Nessa was gone, George's brain ticked over—there *had* to be a way to deal with their problem. She came back, and they walked through to the bar and ordered. Greg opted for a burger—Ineke wouldn't be pleased—and George chose a Pot Noodle with half a loaf of tiger bread. He poured coffees from the machine on the bar, and they sat at a table in the corner, Nessa serving another customer.

"We should get the women moved into flats before offing the men," Greg said.

"Yep, we'll let them know, give them a chance to pack their clothes. The gaffs are all furnished, so it's not like they'll have nothing." Also, the bills and community charge were included in the rent, so there wasn't even electric companies and whatnot for them to deal with. "We have to get the men killed pretty quickly. I don't want anyone worrying about being found and hurt beforehand."

"We'll tell them to stay inside until it's all over. Like we said, assign watchers to keep an eye on the flats. We'll get those tenancy agreements handed over as well."

Nessa came and sat opposite. "Just letting you know, I had to bar someone last night. Not sure if you want to have a word with them."

"Who was it?"

"Phil Rhodes. Usually a pretty unassuming bloke, so her accusation shocked me if I'm honest. Still, he didn't deny it, so…"

"What did he do?"

"Touched a woman up. I'm not saying that's okay because it isn't. Like, he doesn't strike me as an outright pervert."

George's anger ignited. "What the fuck is *wrong* with people? What's her name?"

"Kayla Barnes. She's a regular."

"What sort of bird is she?"

"Young, big eyebrows, orange makeup, fake tanned to within an inch of her life. She cops off with men regularly, she's a massive flirt—I'm not judging, just giving you the info as I see it."

"That's what we like about you." George's annoyance regarding Phil doused a little. If she was a flirt, was this a case of miscommunication between Kayla and Phil? "Do me a favour and send her some flowers from us. Use the business credit card. As for Phil, we'll nip to see him. Give him a little warning." He thought about Nessa's father, Dickie, and how she must have heard of some right scams as she'd been growing up. Dickie had worked for Ron. "While you're here…" He lowered his voice. "I've got something to run past you. Hypothetically, how would you kill several men at once, men who aren't connected in any way except for the fact their other halves know each other?"

"So the police don't twig it's off?"

"Yeah."

"Get them to a party? Send someone in as if they're one of those nutters who do random killing sprees? Then those men just happen to be the ones killed. Actually, there's too much risk to the other people there, so scrap that."

"True, but the random spree thing is a bloody good idea. Cheers."

"Good luck with it." Nessa got up and went back behind the bar. She picked up the phone, presumably to order the flowers.

"Spree killers usually get caught or top themselves afterwards," Greg said.

"Hmm."

"We'll have to find a patsy to do it for us, force them into it. Make out it's an initiation into the firm. Someone who won't be a loss if they shoot themselves."

George stared at him. "Who?"

"Phil Rhodes? He touched a woman without permission. That's enough in my book."

"We need to speak to him and Kayla first. Get both sides of the story."

Their food arrived, bringing the conversation to an end. And that was all right. A Pot Noodle and tiger bread trumped chatter at the minute. George's stomach thought his throat had been cut.

Phil Rhodes, scared out of his mind, trembled so much he was going to piss himself in a minute. The twins stood in front of him at his work—everyone had seen him being brought into the staffroom, and gossip would spread to other floors in the building. The walls seemed to have closed in on him, or maybe it was the size of the blokes that gave the impression there was no air or space left. They'd asked him about Kayla, and he'd responded without hesitation.

"So you pinched her arse," George said. "You actually had the audacity, felt you had the God-given right, to pinch her arse."

"I'm sorry, I thought she fancied me. She'd been flirting, giving out signals. I swear to God I'd never have done it otherwise. It's actually the first time I got the guts up." And that was the truth. He'd always been wary of moving forward with women. "My mate dared me to do it because he knows I haven't got any self-confidence an' that."

George assessed him. "Who's your mate?"

"Jordy Acres."

George seemed surprised. "He's a good kid."

"So am I!"

"I'm surprised he got you to pinch her bum."

"It was just a bit of banter."

"This might end up being a fucking big mistake, but I believe you." George turned to his brother. "What about you?"

"Yep. Words of advice: you need to keep your hands to yourself until it's clear you're allowed to do shit like that. Doing it to a woman the first night you chat to her…not a good idea."

Phil wanted to cry. "I know, I wish I bloody hadn't. I saw straight away it was the wrong thing to do. She slapped me round the face. Bloody hurt, it did. Then she went and told Nessa I'd *rubbed* her arse, then a proper big grope, made it sound worse than it was, and Nessa turfed me out without even asking me if that's what happened. She told me not to come back."

George eyed him. "We'll be in touch."

They walked out, and Phil could breathe again. He so wanted to go up to that bird and tell her the shit she'd got him into by lying. If the twins were going to be in touch, that didn't sound good. What if they visited her next and she spun them some bullshit story and they came back, did him over? She *had* been flirting, even he knew that, despite having little to no experience in that department. He'd watched *Love Island*, for fuck's sake.

What was it she'd said? *I wouldn't mind your hands on me. You can wake up in the morning with me anytime. Have you got a big dick?* You didn't say that sort of thing to someone if you weren't interested, did you? Or was it a joke, she'd led him on for a laugh? He *had* wondered, because she was one of those popular pretty types who usually ignored him.

He left the staffroom and entered the open-plan office, conscious of the stares from his workmates. Great, the Chinese whispers must have started already. He sat at his desk and brought up an Excel spreadsheet, the one he'd been working on not ten minutes ago. The numbers on it blurred.

"I thought you'd come back out of there with a black eye." His colleague at the next desk leaned over. "They didn't look too happy."

Phil laughed to hide his worry. "What, you thought they'd come to beat me up?"

"That's the impression I got."

"Well, you're wrong. I had to give them information, that's all. Something happened at their pub, and I'm a witness."

"Did they pay you? I heard they do that."

Phil was going to have to lie. "A hundred quid."

"Lucky bastard. That's your beer money sorted for Friday night, then."

Phil laughed, although nothing was funny. A visit from those two was never good if they had a bone to pick. He'd be on their radar now. And going out for a beer or two was the last thing on his mind—as were women who said rude shit then cried wolf.

The twins sat in the taxi outside Kayla's work.
"Did you believe her?" Greg asked.
"Nope."

"Me neither. She had that sly look about her when she gave her version of events," George said, "but did you see her face when I said we were going to speak to Phil's mate to double-check her story? Guilty as sin. She led Phil on, then when he reacted, she either had a change of heart or opted to tell Nessa for the fun of it."

"I don't like disbelieving someone when boundaries have been crossed, but in this instance, we're dealing with a vindictive cow."

"Agreed. Let's go and see Jordy. Despite us knowing her name ought to be Bella Bullshit, we finish every job we start. He hasn't got a bad bone in his body, so I can't see him hanging around with someone who has. Yeah, he encouraged Phil, but he isn't the type to be deviant-dodgy."

"What are we going to do if his story matches Phil's?"

"Pay Kayla another visit. Get the truth out of her with a little persuasion."

"You know this leaves us without a patsy, right?"

"Yep, but we'll think of someone to take Phil's place. Come on, get going. We've still got to pop to Haven yet."

Greg drove off, leaving George to wonder why Kayla would want to get Phil into trouble like that. Attention? For warped satisfaction?

"I wish I hadn't told Nessa to buy her those flowers now. We automatically took the woman's side. I need to remember that things aren't always what they seem."

"If Jordy tells us what we think he'll tell us, what's the actual plan with Kayla? I don't want any nasty surprises. I know what you're like."

"A fucking scary warning for now? Mention a Cheshire?"

Greg nodded, and they completed the journey in silence.

Kayla's stomach had dropped when the twins came back. She'd taken them into the staffroom again, and George had asked her to repeat her story. She couldn't remember what she'd said last time, and just her luck, she'd fluffed it up. George had spotted the inconsistency—she'd said he'd groped her tit, not her arse—and then he'd come out with backup info from Jordy.

She'd never been so frightened in all her life. The things George had said to her about lying for kicks to get blokes in trouble… It was a bad habit of hers, chatting bollocks, making things out to be worse than they were, even with women. Mum had always accused her of it, and Dad never believed her these days, even when she *was* telling the truth.

She didn't want her face sliced, like George had promised. And she had to give some flowers to her mum when they arrived. Apparently, Kayla didn't deserve them now.

Chapter Sixteen

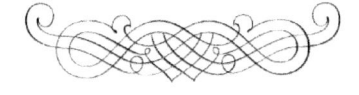

Saturday evening had rolled around, and Quenton had never felt so free—and justified. Knowing Ulysses couldn't hurt him again and had paid with his life for what he'd done was the comfort he'd needed for many years. Who'd have thought that contributing to someone's death would bring such happiness?

In the days since, he'd thought about how he'd once loved that man so much, endless amounts, and how, at the height of their relationship, just the thought of Vincent leaving him had brought on tears and a sick-inducing fear that he'd never be able to be his true self with anyone else. How quickly things had changed, Quenton watching the rise to fame from the sidelines, the adulation, being left behind to hide in the shadows of Vincent's former life, a phantom who no longer mattered. And then finding out who'd sent the letters. Any lingering strands of love that had remained had fizzled into nothing but pure hatred.

It had hit the news, the famous actor who'd gone missing, and the speculation had escalated. All those keyboard detectives on the internet, dishing out theories, convinced they knew what had happened. Every former lover coming out of the woodwork to clear their names, typing into their status boxes where they'd been on the night Ulysses King had last been seen.

Would the police speak to Quenton? If they hadn't already, it must mean he wasn't a person of interest. Barely anyone had known about his affair with Ulysses anyway, and there wasn't an official record of him living at the townhouse, but that was the route Quenton would take if one of Ulysses' friends from back in the day happened to mention it: Ulysses had stayed there for a while as a tenant, and Quenton had known him as Vincent.

But what if Ulysses had told someone Quenton owned the house and they'd been lovers? What if he *had* let someone know he was coming to the manor the other night? What if he'd left his phone in the car, despite saying he hadn't brought it, and the police would see his last location, or thereabouts?

George had assured Quenton that the bank transfer would point to exactly what they wanted it to—an innocent payment for chips at their casino, Jackpot Palace, ones he'd borrowed to play roulette, the twins trusting him to pay up later on.

That might go wrong, though. Something was bound to. Luck had never been on Quenton's side, his life a series of savage experiences, one after the other—and he included a wretched childhood in that, his father a strict bastard, his mother never sticking up for her son.

There was no need to fret, he reminded himself, it was all in hand. A young man who worked for the twins had come to collect Ulysses' car while they'd been in the steel room and would have searched the interior for a mobile and switched it off far away from here—at a point beside the Thames, apparently. The car itself had a new set of plates attached, then he'd driven it to the crusher. The only thing to worry about was any ANPR cameras picking it up on the way *here*, giving the police an idea of where Ulysses had gone, and if the phone *had* been on, it might show he'd been in this area.

"But the main road is used by many," he muttered George's words, "he could have just been driving past." He lit a cigarette and wished he could be as nonchalant, as self-assured as George. "Come on now, stop being silly. The police haven't contacted you. The thugs have fixed everything."

He sipped whiskey, and the sudden sound of a vehicle coming up the driveway almost had him throwing the glass in shock. He couldn't see any headlights, the drawing room curtains were too thick, so he stubbed his cigarette out, got up, and walked to the window. Parted the curtains and peered out.

No car.

Had he imagined the noise of that engine and the gravel crunching beneath the tyres? Surely not. He was getting on in years, but his hearing hadn't failed him yet. He downed his drink, returning the glass to the side table. Had they parked out the back?

Quenton dashed as fast as he was able to the sitting room. He hadn't closed the curtains in there so sidled in the darkness to the French doors, keeping to the side of them. He squinted outside.

"Oh, what the devil do *they* want?"

Chapter Seventeen

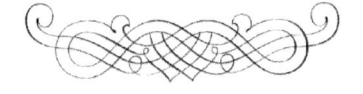

Nora tugged the bell rope. This was it. The night they'd get Quenton out of their hair for good. She looked forward to a life where he wasn't in the back of her mind, lurking there as a threat. But then again, he still would be. His death would be. The fear of capture would be.

They'd used the back roads from Margate to avoid cameras as much as possible, Nora doctoring her numberplate with black tape. They already knew what they were going to say if their faces got caught on camera: they'd come back to London because Nora had forgotten her phone. She'd left it at home exactly for that reason. Lucia had left hers in the caravan. They'd also settled on a method of murder. Suffocation. It was the cleanest way to do it, Nora putting a pillow on Quenton's face and sitting on it.

The door opened, and he stood in the murky half-darkness of the corridor, light from the foyer only touching the far end of the flagstone floor.

"What are you two doing back here?" he snapped.

Affronted, Nora glared at him. "You're talking to me like that after what I arranged for you with the twins? Bloody cheeky bastard. Is that any way to treat someone who helped you out of a sticky spot?"

"I suppose, but it's not advisable that you're here. You must have seen the news. What if the police come here tonight and see you? What will we say?"

"That we're friends and I was with you the evening he was killed, all right? Don't worry yourself about it."

He seemed to calm down. "I still don't understand why you've come."

"We fancied a chat to make sure we're all on the same page."

He stepped back, turned, and ambled down the corridor.

"Kitchen," he called over his shoulder. "I haven't eaten yet."

That's annoying. There aren't any sodding pillows in there.

Nora glanced at Lucia and whispered, "Fucking hell, we'll have to get him into the sitting room later."

They both had gloves on, their hair tucked beneath woolly hats, and entered the house, Nora locking the door behind them. In the kitchen, Quenton prodded at the transparent casing of a ready meal with the tip of a knife. He put it on the worktop, shoved the tray in the microwave, and set it to four minutes.

"Would you like a cup of tea?" he asked.

Lucia subtly shook her head at Nora, perhaps worrying about them leaving their DNA around the rims of the cups, but that was easily solved by washing them. *Not* having a drink while they were supposedly here for a 'chat' would arouse Quenton's suspicions.

"Please," she said.

Lucia pursed her lips, and Quenton turned his back to switch on the kettle.

Lucia perched at the large pine table where the staff used to sit to eat their lunch. God, this place dragged out so many memories, some good, some not so good, but coming here, even though Nora had hated the job, had been a respite from her home life with Oscar.

Quenton took three of the best china cups and saucers from the cupboard, the ones Darcy had reserved for guests they wanted to impress. Royal Doulton.

"I'm surprised you're using those," Nora said.

"Darcy and Cook aren't here to tell me not to, and besides, there are only four remaining. I broke the others over the years."

"Did you miss Darcy, you know, after?" Nora asked.

"No."

"What about her boys?"

"No."

"I suppose you were too busy having a good time with Ulysses, all those holidays and whatnot." She hated him for being able to do that. He had the cover of being rich so could swan off whenever he liked. Nora would have loved to have gone abroad, but it would have raised some eyebrows as to how she could afford it. "Did you ever wonder, or find out, why he called himself Mr Orchid?"

"I didn't, and it's always bothered me, not knowing if it was significant or not." He spooned tea leaves into the exact same pot that had been in this house years ago. They'd made things to last back then. "I wondered if it was because they're considered exotic flowers—he certainly thought *he* was exotic. He was born in Japan, you know. His parents lived there for a time. He came to London when he was five."

"So how did it all go? The murder, I mean."

Quenton poured milk into a little jug then brought it and a bowl of sugar cubes over. Silver tongs perched on top of the white squares, yet again a remnant from the past. He carried the teapot across, placing it on a metal trivet, then collected his food from the microwave. How weird that he'd continued the tradition where serving tea was concerned, keeping up appearances and remaining in a bygone age, yet ate out of a plastic tray that brought him right into modern times.

He pondered, then landed on: "It was…exhilarating."

Exhilarating? Fucking hell, he really is a mean fucker.

"So you enjoyed it, then? Can't say I did when you told me to kill your wife and those kiddies, but each to their own." Nora sniffed in disdain. *She* wouldn't be exhilarated when she killed Quenton, more like relieved on one hand that he wasn't around to get them into trouble, and also scared to death that their alibi would crumble. The times wouldn't match up where they left London to go back to Margate because they'd stopped off here, but she could say she'd driven slowly, given it was night-time, couldn't she?

"You really can't get over that, can you?" He forked up a wedge of unidentifiable food that Lucia appeared to be disgusted by. Cauliflower cheese? Something pale anyway.

"I've thought about it a lot over the years," Nora went on. "How quickly you were prepared for them to die. As if you'd planned it all along, to use me to do it. The power you had over me as my boss, you used that to your advantage. Yes, I could have said no, but I was young, didn't have the balls I do now. If the same thing happened today, I'd have killed *you* instead."

What she'd said lingered in the air between them.

Quenton ate as though she hadn't uttered that last line, as if he didn't *believe* she had the guts to do it. Her hatred for him grew, and she eyed the knife. Would it be so bad if she snatched it up? Grabbed his hair from behind and slit his throat? She'd get hardly any blood on her that way.

"I just want something cleared up," she said. "You're obviously an arsehole, you don't care who you hurt to get what you want, and you've denied it already, but for once, just be truthful. *Did* you get Edie and Margo killed?"

He'd eaten his dinner quickly and got up to put the fork in the sink and the tray in the bin. "What would you say if I had? Hypothetically, of course."

"I'd say you're a bigger bastard than I thought you were, a man with zero feelings for anyone but himself. That you didn't trust them to keep the robbery a secret so the only alternative was to get rid of them."

He turned from the bin and smiled at her, almost as if he didn't see her, only whatever memories played out in his head. "I didn't trust you two either."

Was that an admission, only he wasn't outright saying it?

Nora's stomach rolled over. "Funny thing is, *we* trusted *you*."

And they had. He'd stuck to the planned story back then, so none of them had any reason to think he'd grass them up—because saying they were the robbers would have implicated him, too. They'd all agreed that if he opened his trap, they'd blame it on him.

"Let me tell you something." He sat at the table again. "Seeing as you want honesty, I'll give it to you, then we'll go our separate ways and *never* see each other again."

"Go on then—if you can even *be* honest, which I highly doubt."

"Yes, I wanted Darcy and her children gone. I was living a complete lie just to please my father, and I *did* use you to…dispatch them. It wasn't planned, though, and I say that with all sincerity.

It came to me on the night, when Darcy realised who you were. I couldn't risk her saying something. No amount of persuasion on my part would have worked, you know what she was like. It was better for all concerned that she was out of the picture. She would have told the police about you, and we'd have all been arrested eventually. The children...I couldn't trust that they wouldn't tell the police either."

"Thank you for that, telling the truth—I suspected it all along anyway. Now on to Edie and Margo."

"I suppose I can he honest there, too. It's not like you can do anything about it, is it." He laughed. "I can't see you wanting to confess and go to prison at your age, just so I end up there, too. Please understand that I panicked and thought...well, I thought that erasing you all would mean I could live without that constant fear. I thought you'd told them I was a homosexual. So yes, I arranged their deaths."

Anger roiled inside Nora, so bitter she swore it produced an acidic taste on her tongue. "But you had a loose end, someone else to kill if you'd have succeeded in murdering me and Lucia—the person you used to do it. What, did you kill *him*, too? And why didn't you keep sending him after us two?"

"I realised you weren't going to say anything after all. The rational side of me kicked in. As the years passed, I calmed down, and besides, he died and I had no one else to help me. And here we are."

Lucia shrieked, grabbed the knife, and got up, lunging towards him. She shoved him off the chair, and he fell to the floor, screeching. He rolled over onto his stomach to push himself up, but Lucia dived on him, sitting on his legs. She raised the knife.

"No," Nora shouted. "Think of the blood."

But it seemed Lucia was too far gone. She brought the blade down and sank it into his back—and kept repeating the motion until scarlet dotted the floor, her clothes, her face. Nora stared on in horror, remaining rooted to her chair with Quenton's screams barking all around her, too loud. Her stomach revolted at the sight, the *smell*. She heaved, slapping a hand to her mouth, her mind ticking over too fast—the state of the floor, any fibre transfer from Lucia's clothes to his, a strand of her hair falling from beneath the hat, the police finding one tiny clue that would link her to this...

Link me... Oh fuck.

Lucia got up and backed away. Dropped the knife as if only now realising she'd wielded it. She turned to Nora, her face spotted with red, thick freckles that dripped down her skin. "I... Oh God, what have I done?"

Exactly what I asked myself back then.

Lucia shook, hugging herself, her bottom lip quivering, and all Nora could think was: *Don't come near me. I don't want that blood on me.* And: *It's going to make a mess in my car. The police are going to know.*

"You stupid cow!" Nora shouted. "What the fuck are we supposed to do now?"

"I don't know," Lucia wailed. "He killed our *friends*, he wanted to kill *us*. I got so angry I just—"

"I know, I get it, but we agreed on a pillow, not a fucking knife."

Lucia sobbed, bringing her hands up to her face, the black gloves covering her expression of shame and fear. There was only one thing for it, something Nora didn't want to do, but what choice did they have?

"Listen to me," she said.

Lucia dragged her hands away, smearing the blood on her cheeks.

"We have to get our stories straight one last time, do you understand?"

Lucia nodded.

Nora got her thoughts in order. "Right, I'm going to have to bring the twins in on this—don't say no, they're the only hope we have. This is how it went: we were reminiscing in Margate, okay, and we thought about Edie and Margo dying, how *we* nearly died, and we realised what Quenton had done. We couldn't let it lie so came back to London. We asked him, and he admitted it. You lost your rag, and now he's dead. That's it—keep it simple. If they ask why we happened to have hats and gloves on indoors, we're old, we get cold easily. Whether they'll believe that is anyone's guess, but it's the best reason we've got. We didn't *plan* to kill him, got it? That knife is his, it was on the table, so that isn't a lie. Have you got all that?"

Lucia nodded again.

"Repeat it to me," Nora said.

Lucia went through it all and, satisfied she wasn't going to fuck it up when the twins got here, if they even agreed to help them, Nora had a terrible thought. Her phone was at home. Lucia's was in Margate. Quenton still had a house phone, but there was no way she could use that.

What the hell were they going to do?

Nora scrabbled for a solution. Thankfully, one popped up to save them. "You're going to have to stay here—you can wait for me outside if you don't want to be near him, but keep to the back of the house so people going by in cars don't see you. The people at the Gables are in Poland, so you're all right there. I'm the only one without blood on me, so it won't get in my car—I have to go home to ring the twins."

Lucia cried, shaking her head. "I can't stay..."

Nora wanted to slap her. "You can—you *have* to. If you want to get away with this, that's how it's got to be. We're going to walk out of here now, and you're not going to touch anything. Even outside, you don't lean on the wall, nothing. You'll stand there and won't move. Do. You. Understand. Me?"

"Yes." Lucia hiccupped. "*Yes!*"

"Good."

Nora sighed, the exhalation juddery. "You'd better hope George and Greg agree to come here, otherwise we're royally fucked."

Chapter Eighteen

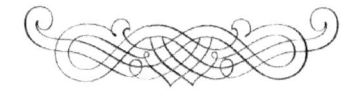

Nora had crept out the back way again to go and see Pinocchio so Roger thought she was still at home. He'd caught her as she'd arrived back from the manor but hadn't questioned her about the car disappearing. Instead, he'd wanted to talk about how to go about getting a cat as he fancied one for company.

"Her down the road's got a litter of tabbies," she'd said. "They're ready to go now, so you'd best get there before they're snapped up. You'll have to pay for it, mind."

"Well, I wouldn't expect one for free. Where do I need to go?"

"Sally's at number three."

He'd bustled off down the street. At least if he was kept busy entertaining a kitten he'd be less interested in what Nora was doing.

The two-bus journey to Essex with the jewellery in her bag had given her a big dose of anxiety. Paranoid, she'd imagined everyone stared at her, that they could somehow see through the leather to what she carried inside. She'd worried someone would snatch the bag, then everything would have been in vain.

In a side street off the main thoroughfare, she stood outside Pinocchio's. Butterflies rioted in her belly, and she wanted to be sick. Several people had come and gone, and now the shop was empty apart from the owner himself.

She walked in, the tinkling bell a rasp on her nerves—it seemed too loud in announcing her arrival. Locking the door behind her, she approached the counter. Pinocchio eyed her knowingly. Maybe people who had a lot of gear to fence always locked the door, too. Bag on the counter, she took a large breath and prepared her speech, but he spoke first.

"Don't worry, you're safe. When we've conducted business and parted ways, you weren't even here, understand? I've never seen you before in my life."

She nodded. Had a good look at him. Thin. Ratty. A suit as black as his slicked-back hair. White shirt, a gaudy paisley tie. Spindly fingers that flickered, spiders' legs, and she shuddered.

"Even if I can't help you, if you catch my drift, you can walk out of here knowing our discussion won't be repeated."

Despite him matching every wheeler and dealer she'd ever encountered in the East End, that self-confident air about him, she thought he was telling the truth.

She blew out a breath. "Um, there was a robbery in London last night."

"Yep, if it was Goosemoor, I've already heard about it. News like that travels fast. I've had plod in here earlier this morning, asking me to keep an eye out for certain pieces. No need to look panicked, I won't be saying jack shit if they come back."

"I've been asked to—"

"—sell the goods." He tutted, then said, as if to himself, "Why do these outfits always send a woman?"

"I don't know."

"Probably because you're less likely to be suspected as a fence. Go and pull the blinds, there's some nosy tart looking at the window display."

Nora returned to the door, doing as he'd said, worrying the woman would remember her later down the line if it all went tits up. She moved to the window to repeat the process, thankful the window-shopper didn't look up at her. Back at the counter, she did indeed feel safe—or safer—without the feeling that people outside stared at her back.

Pinocchio smiled wide. "Word on the street is it was a big haul."

She nodded.

"Let's have a look then."

She took each jewellery case out of the bag and laid them on the counter. Pinocchio opened them one by one, peering at the stones through what looked like a mini telescope. It took an age, him humming and nodding, her shaking and wanting to scream. Several people knocked on the door, and he shouted that he was closed until later. Finally, he pulled a notepad across and named each piece, a brief description of them, then a price.

Nora almost fainted from shock. "Is that...is that what you'd give me for it all, or does your cut need to be taken off first?"

"That's the price I'm offering you. It's worth a fuck lot more, obviously, but as they carry a risk, I deserve to make some cash on the deal."

She'd expected some bullshit like that anyway. Everyone who'd heard of Pinocchio was aware he shafted customers. But there was way more than the five grand Quenton needed, more than she thought the dealer would give her. Nora and her mates would be set for years. Going home on the bus with all that money was far more daunting than the journey with the jewellery, but she'd have to do it.

"I need to visit the bank," he said. "I don't have that amount of dosh on the premises, as you can imagine." He smiled. "Go and have a cuppa somewhere. Come back in two hours." He popped each case back in her bag.

"Why two hours? Where the hell's your bank?"

"Up the road, but you can bet they'll need to get some more cash from other branches."

"I see. I can't walk around town with all that, though, it was bad enough getting on the bus with it," she said but at the same time didn't want to leave the jewellery there. He could steal it, and when she got

back, he might make out they'd never had this conversation—and there'd be nothing she could do about it.

"If you think I'm in the habit of nicking off people, think again. I do drive a hard bargain, but my rep's stellar, ask anyone."

"I didn't think—"

"Yes, you did, it was written all over your face, and you'd be a strange bird if you didn't worry, seeing as you're not from around here and you don't know me, although I'm well known outside of Essex, too. I must be, else you wouldn't be here. Did someone recommend me?"

"The robbers told me to come."

"There you go then, I'm famous." He chuckled, took a receipt book off the side of the till, and wrote MISCELLANEOUS GOODS, *adding an IOU and the payment at the bottom. He signed it, ripped the sheet off, and handed it to her. "I'm good for my word. Like I said, two hours."*

He took the cases back out and turned to a huge safe in the wall behind him. Unlocked it. Stacks of money and other boxes sat inside. He turned to her. "Avoid the Shepherd and Lamb in the high street. People are nosy there, they'll notice you're not a local."

Nora rushed to the door, wishing she'd come in her car. The idea of going back on the busses with all that money frightened her. She left the shop, going across the street to a different pub and sitting in the top-right corner, her back to the other customers so they couldn't study her face. A woman took her order—a ploughman's and a pot of tea—and Nora stared at the blank wall, evaluating her life since the rent man and Ron's thug had come calling.

This time last week she'd been living a miserable existence, hating her husband and wishing she had an escape route. She bloody well had one now, only it was loaded with danger and the high risk she'd end up in prison. But no, her alibi had checked out, and there was no reason whatsoever for anyone to suspect her.

Her lunch arrived. She ate, the cheese too thick, the pickled onions too sharp. She felt less shaky after eating, though, and the tea was good. A check of her watch told her she still had an hour and twenty minutes to wait. What if the bank questioned Pinocchio about why he was withdrawing that much money? Or, because of his business, were they used to him taking vast quantities out? Going by the amount of cash in the safe, they were certainly used to him depositing it. He hadn't seemed worried about going there, so maybe she shouldn't be either.

Time crawled by. She'd managed to get three cups out of the teapot, then bought another one. She now needed the loo. She got up and followed the sign with an arrow, coming out into a passage with two doors, pictures of a man and woman on their fronts. She did a wee, washed her hands, and caught sight of herself in the speckled mirror above the sink. She looked ill—as well she might—but that could be passed off as her being upset about Oscar.

Everything would be all right, she had to believe that. She planned to keep her portion of the cash under her bed and put some in the bank every week as if it were her wages. She'd feel better once she had a safe.

She thrust it all out of her mind—she needed the quiet of home in order to think it through properly— and ordered a slice of Victoria sponge to waste the remaining minutes. Then she left the pub and entered the pawnshop. Another customer browsed some knick-knacks to the right, and she glanced at Pinocchio who jerked a thumb to a door behind the counter. She scooted through into a back room stacked with cardboard boxes, general pawned household paraphernalia, and an armchair with a little table beside it. She sat, the tinkle of the bell heralding yet another customer had come in or maybe the current one was leaving.

The door opened. "All clear." Pinocchio gestured for her to go back into the shop.

She stood on the other side of the counter. "I need you to put the money in batches."

"A share for each robber? I get you."

She explained how the jewellery had been divvied so he could add up the five totals.

"I thought there were only four armed men?"

"One portion is mine for fencing. Five grand."

"Blimey, you're getting a fair old whack."

It took some time for him to count it all while she watched. All those notes, more than she'd ever seen in her life. Would the interest from the bank be enough for her to stretch it out for the rest of her life when she'd finally deposited it in small increments? No, with inflation changing over the coming years, it wouldn't be worth as much as it was today. Maybe she could tell the landlord she'd come into life insurance money because of Oscar and ask if she could buy the house. She had more than enough to do that. She could buy two if she chose to, rent one out and still have a load left over. She'd have a steady stream of income then, on top of her new job at the factory.

Pinocchio took some brown paper bags from beneath the counter and placed each batch of money inside.

Nora lifted a pen out of an old cup by the till and put an initial on each so she didn't get them mixed up.

"This lot isn't going to fit in your bag," he said.

Shit, she hadn't thought of that.

Pinocchio scooted around the counter and went straight for a leather suitcase standing beside a fancy set of stacked dining chairs. "This'll cost you."

Nora nodded and opened her purse, handing over the price he quoted.

He put the bags into the case for her, zipped it up, and smiled. "Pleasure doing business with you. If it makes you feel better, when I heard about the robbery, I already got a buyer lined up, just in case. Must have had a premonition you'd turn up. Look, you don't seem well. Are you all right?"

She nodded. "I've never done anything like this before."

"Bit stupid of them to trust the haul with a novice, but what do I know? Out of curiosity, where's the ruby-and-diamond set, the one in the papers?"

"I don't know."

"Just seems a bit weird to me that they didn't nick that an' all."

"I was just told to bring stuff here. I didn't get told anything else."

Her mind now zipped to the fact she had to heft a case onto the busses and somehow get it inside her house without anyone seeing. Wanting to cry—this was so hard*—she hung her handbag strap across her body and lugged the case to the door. Fumbling with the lock, her fingers turning to sausages, she eventually went out onto the street. No one paid her any mind—after all, she could have just bought the suitcase to go on holiday—so she walked to the bus stop and waited.*

Every second that passed seemed elongated. Every stare she received brought on a flutter of panic. The bus arrived, and she got on, sitting at the back, the case wedged between her legs.

Calm down.

Ten minutes later, she switched to the bus that would take her to London. All the way there, she fretted. She took a cab from the bus station instead of walking, asking the driver to drop her off in the street behind hers. She rushed through her back garden, went inside, and dropped the case on the kitchen floor. Door locked, she cried, so relieved to be home.

But it wasn't over yet. She still had to get Quenton's money to him.

She nipped to the toilet, made a cuppa, and sat to gather her wits. Go through everything she'd done today to spot potential pitfalls. Surely she hadn't been memorable enough in the pub for someone to link her to the sale of the jewellery—and why the hell would they anyway? Pinocchio had likely handed the goods to the buyer already and laughed to himself about the hefty profit. The proof of the stolen items was gone, so if she could just get her mind to stop throwing out ridiculous scenarios regarding her getting caught, that would be great.

Tea finished, she phoned the manor, ending the call after three rings, the prearranged signal so Quenton knew to pick it up instead of Patty when it rang again. She dialled a second time, holding her breath.

"Lord Goosemoor," he said.

"It's done."

"Oh, thank God. Go to the agreed place. I'll be there in twenty minutes."

Nora put the receiver in the cradle and dragged the case upstairs. She took Quenton's paper bag out and shoved the case under her bed. Downstairs, she stashed his money in her large wicker shopping bag and left the house, driving to the rendezvous spot.

Quenton was already there.

Nora took his share from the bag, got out, and went to his car. His window was already down, so she handed the cash to him.

"Work tomorrow," he said.

"I'm aware of that, but I've got another job. I'll be leaving in a month."

"I beg your pardon!"

"You heard."

She flounced off and drove away, her mind on tonight. She'd invite Margo, Edie, and Lucia round for another booze-up. They'd get their money, meet up again every month to keep appearances the same as usual, but it would never be the same. They'd made it clear what they thought of her for killing Darcy and the boys. Maybe, given time, the shock of that would fade and they'd return to some semblance of normality in their friendship. Nora doubted it, though. She'd forever be a killer in their eyes.

Now she had to visit Ron to return the gun and give him that favour for the balaclavas. Could this day get any worse?

She put gloves on and took the shooter out of the larder where she'd hidden it behind some flour, popping it in her handbag. In the car, she drove to Ron's 'office' and tapped on the door. Sam opened it, frowned, but let her in.

"Nip down to the café for a couple of bacon butties, will you?" Ron said to him.

Sam frowned some more and left.

"Lock the door and close the blinds," Ron ordered.

Shaking, Nora did as she was told and turned to face the desk.

Ron lounged behind it, taking a sip of amber liquid from a crystal glass. "He can get a bit confused, can Sam. He'll trot off now, wondering if I told him earlier you were coming. He'll think he forgot, worry that he forgot. Then he'll come back, find the door locked while you do me that agreed favour, and he'll call through to check if I'm all right. I'll say yes then squeeze your throat tighter, and he'll wait until you open the door and fuck off out of here. I take it you brought the gun."

Nora took it out of her bag—realising too late she still had gloves on from when she'd put it in there. Gloves, in June. A fucking giveaway something was up, something people might have noticed if they'd looked out of their windows when she'd left her house.

"What did you do with the balaclavas?" he asked.

"I burnt them."

She handed the weapon to him. He casually polished it with a rag, staring at her all the while. She blushed under his scrutiny, wishing he'd just get on with it and take what he wanted.

And then he did.

Chapter Nineteen

In forensic gear, George and Greg stood in the kitchen at the manor. What a fucking mess—they'd have to get a cleaning crew in to go over every part of the ground floor, just to be on the safe side. Nora had stayed at home, per George's instructions, to burn her clothes, gloves, and shoes in her fireplace, then she was back off to

Margate, returning tomorrow as originally planned. If her nosy fucker of a next-door neighbour questioned her on why she'd gone home, she'd use the original excuse of collecting her phone.

As for Lucia… When they'd arrived, they'd coasted along the driveway with their headlights off, parked the van by the walled enclosure, then found her by some French doors, a gibbering wreck. Greg had given her a flagon of water from the van to wash her face and hair with once she'd stripped, their backs turned to her for privacy, then she'd got dressed in a forensic suit and currently sat barefoot in the back. She was likely cold, but there was sod all that could be done about it.

Greg would burn her clothes when they got home. Lucia was going to stay with them, and Debbie was bringing new clothes round for her in the morning. Dropping Lucia off at Haven tonight when she was meant to be in Margate wasn't advisable. There were too many people there who'd query why she'd come back early. George had warned her that if she ever told anyone where they lived, they'd have to shut her up—he'd left it up to her whether she took that as murder or her tongue being cut out. Cruel of him, but he had to protect himself and Greg over her. She was aware of the score anyway as she knew exactly what went on at Haven and that the abusers were going to be sorted.

Nora's panicked phone call was the last thing they'd needed at the end of a long day, one where they'd moved the last woman into a flat and still hadn't settled on a patsy. At last, there were a few candidates on the list, random people who were on their second warnings from previous offences on Cardigan turf, so now they were whittling them down to the ones who'd obey the command to go on a shooting spree without question. Of course, they wouldn't be told they'd be killed afterwards to make it look like suicide, but that was neither here nor there.

"Lucia was angry, wasn't she," George muttered, eyeing Quenton's back, the ripped shirt where the blade had sliced through. "The amount stab marks… A lot of pent-up frustration there."

Greg sighed. "Wouldn't *you* be angry, though? He killed two of her friends and tried to off her and Nora. What an absolute wanker."

"I wonder if he used the bloke he contacted for the robbery to do his dirty work for him with Margo and Edie. He said he was dead now, but he could still have been alive when they were killed. I didn't ask Nora when it happened."

"Maybe. We'll never know because *he's* bloody dead an' all."

George loved killing, but other people found it immensely difficult—obviously, because they weren't nutters like him. "D'you reckon Lucia will be all right? I mean, killing someone is a sodding big thing. Shall we get her to go and see Vic for a bit of therapy?"

"Might be advisable."

George sniffed. "Right, we'll load him in the van—she'll just have to get over sharing the back with a dead body. It's best he goes to the warehouse. I'll chop him up and dump him in the Thames. We'll need two crews, one here, one at the warehouse for after."

Greg tsked. "I know."

"I'm just saying it out loud so I've got it straight in my head." George imagined the fallout from tonight. "This is going to create a stink in the news, *two* old boys going missing. Maybe the coppers will make a connection between them after all and assume they've run off together."

"With neither of them using their bank or credit cards? I doubt it."

"Didn't think of that."

George went to the sitting room and brought a large rug into the kitchen. They rolled the body up in it, carrying it outside between them, the head end on George's shoulder, the feet on Greg's. Lucia shrieked when George opened the back door of the van and they loaded the corpse inside.

"I get that you're freaked out, love, but this is *your* doing, so cut it out, all right?"

She shuffled up to the backs of the front seats, hugging her knees, her forehead resting on them. George felt for her, poor old dear, but if you were going to get arsey and kill someone, you had to get on and live with it. They'd keep an eye on her once she went back to work at Haven. If it seemed like she needed another warning to act normally, George had no qualms about giving it. Getting heavy with her wasn't something he wanted to do, but sometimes their job required it.

They left the back door of the manor unlocked. George sent the main crew a message, telling them no headlights and to park round the back. Later, the manor would appear as if Nora and Lucia had never been there, but the strong scent of chemicals would be a big clue that the place had been sanitised. Depending on how social Quenton had been, maybe no one would realise he was missing for a while, so when the police arrived, that smell might be gone.

George secured the van door and got in the passenger seat. All he and Greg could do was ensure loose ends were tied off. A bit like Quenton had tried to do, except it had failed and, years later, he'd died because of it.

Stupid cunt. He should have just moved on after the robbery. Serves himself right.

Chapter Twenty

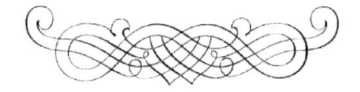

Anaisha had been given the task of making friends with Flint and reporting anything iffy about him back to the twins. An easy job, considering what Janine did for them. So far, there had been nothing Anaisha would class as a reason to grass him up. Since she'd agreed to work for them, that had been her only instruction, apart from going to the meeting about the abusive men. She'd already said she'd be no good to them in other areas, seeing as she only worked on the Internet Crime team and her fucking about with police files would get noticed—her boss was a lurker. She supposed her inclusion in the meeting at the back of the Noodle and Tiger was their way of reminding her she belonged to them now. She didn't *need* a reminder, she *wanted* to be in their firm—well, she did now she'd got used to it. She'd had time to think about her new place in the world and why she'd become a police officer, and if getting justice meant she was also a cog in a gangland organisation, then so be it.

Her murdered brother, Dayton, would have been ashamed of her, as would her parents if they ever found out. She'd been brought up to be a good girl, law-abiding and kind, but Dayton's death had changed her. Dark thoughts had visited, still did, turning her into someone she didn't recognise anymore, someone she was getting to know. On the outside she was nice and innocent, but on the inside, a monster lurked.

There was no going back, not since she'd asked for two men to be offed—Dayton's killer, Shaq, and her ex-boyfriend, Ben. She'd stepped way too far over the line to ever be able to return to who she'd been before.

She didn't even want to go back. She'd made peace with who she was becoming. It helped to have Janine to chat to about it, and Flint when he was in the right mood. Janine had led Dayton's case, and they'd grown close—or as close as Janine would allow someone to get.

Anaisha stood outside Flint's flat, having messaged to ask him if he fancied a few drinks. He hadn't seemed to want her tagging on to him the other times she'd asked to get together, likely only agreeing because the twins had told him he had to mentor her, same as Janine had mentored him. She understood why George and Greg wanted her to root around to find some dirt on Flint—he was an odd man, always looked guarded outside of work and acted as if he had something to hide. At the station he was completely different, everyone's friend. The two sides of him didn't make sense. Anaisha had a handle on disguising her true self, she'd had enough time to perfect it, but it seemed Flint hadn't mastered it yet. Maybe that was just him being grumpy because he'd been forced to work for George and Greg, but it wasn't a good look, not if the twins needed to trust him.

Flint had agreed to her coming over tonight, but only after she'd said she'd bring a bottle of alcohol, plus she'd pay for a takeaway. It could be a fair while before he opened up to her, but that was okay, she could play the long game. She'd done it with Shaq, visiting him in prison for years, waiting for the opportunity to kill him, and she could do it again now.

She tapped on the door, and Flint let her in, his body language and expression saying it was somewhat begrudgingly, although his eyes lit up at her holding aloft a large bottle of elderflower-flavoured gin. She ordered a Chinese and set about getting him to slip up, to reveal hidden parts of himself she could pass on to George and Greg, but he remained in control despite drinking four large gins.

Two hours later, he got up to use the toilet, something she'd been waiting for. She'd spied a laptop on the coffee table as soon as she'd entered the living room, the screen winking out just as she'd sat on the sofa. Flint had closed it casually, giving her no reason to think he was hiding anything, but, considering she'd spotted another laptop down the side of his chair, she was now curious as to what he'd been doing prior to her arrival. Even though it was probably innocent—the second laptop could be for work—she reached across and lifted the lid, tapping the touchpad. A white cursor darted across the dark screen a second before the internet page he'd been on sprang to life.

She stared at it, shocked to her bones. The header seemed to scream at her: LONDON TEENS. She tried to convince herself he was only on there to catch perverts—they'd all been desperate to find Fishy_For_Life, Anaisha tasked with the job at work to talk to someone online who'd claimed to be a boy but in reality had been a paedo. But Kendall Reynolds had been found by Flint, offed by Terry Meeks, the father of a girl called Summer who'd killed herself because Fishy had threatened to put intimate pictures of her all over social media.

So why was Flint on London Teens if the pervert had been sorted?

And why did he have a chat box open, his username London_Lad?

Had the twins told him to go on the site to trip up any more pervs who could be lurking? That made sense.

Quickly, she scrolled through the conversation. At one point yesterday, Flint had said he'd stopped going on Teens but had come back—he'd missed it. The last of his messages sent her stone-cold, goosebumps sprouting.

London_Lad: Got any pics of you naked?

Best_Girl: OMG! You're well rude.

*IMG 0005_0000

Best_Girl: You still there?

Best_Girl: Helloooooooooo?

Best_Girl: Ignore me then. I don't care.

Anaisha checked the time stamp in the box. He'd sent that request for a photo just before she'd arrived. Had he been desperate to respond the whole time she'd been there? Instead of him listening to what she'd been saying, had his mind been on a teenager and whether she'd sent him a picture?

Filthy fucking bastard. And that poor girl…

The sound of the toilet flushing churned her stomach, and she closed the laptop lid, sitting back and shutting her eyes, acting as if the gin and food had turned her sleepy. But her mind spun, nausea paying her a harsh visit, and she battled not to be sick.

Flint was a paedo.

Flint had lied to them.

Flint had possibly framed Kendall Reynolds.

She judged when he'd come into the room and opened her eyes. "Bloody hell, I almost dropped off then." Had she sounded normal enough?

He chuckled and sat in the armchair. "I just had a cheeky poo. I hate it when you don't know one's coming, then it surprises you."

That explained why he'd been in the bathroom long enough for her to be nosy, but bloody hell, did he have to tell her that? "Err, too much information, mate."

"Sorry."

"I need a wee, but I'm not going in there after you." She sat forward. "I'd best be getting home anyway. Thanks for letting me come round. We'll have to do it again sometime."

She got up and slipped her coat on. Flint appeared pleased she was leaving—*I bet he fucking is*—and showed her out. What should she do? Ring Oliver, her boss, so he could contact the owner of the website, or tell the twins?

She stood round the side of the building. She'd got a taxi here, what with her drinking, so she'd have to text whoever from here. A quick recall of what she'd been told to do in circumstances where Cardigan residents were involved, and she knew she'd have to get hold of The Brothers. She took her burner phone out. Inhaled a deep breath.

A: Been round F's tonight. Looked on his laptop—he's got two. A window was open for London Teens. He's talking to a girl about naked pics.

GG: You fucking what?

A: Did you give him that job?

GG: No we bloody didn't!

A: Shit. What if Kendall was telling the truth and he wasn't Fishy?

GG: Jesus Christ. Where are you?

A: Round the side of F's flat.

GG: Go home.

A: Will do. Need to call a cab first.

GG: Actually, no, wait there. We'll pick you up in the taxi.

Anaisha leaned on the wall in the darkness, sick to her stomach. She'd bet the twins would get her to go back to Flint's with them. She'd have her first real job as their copper, helping them kill him. Because Flint wouldn't be allowed to live, not now. There was no legitimate reason whatsoever for him to ask for a nude pic.

But they surprised her. They drove her away and let her in on the plan they'd come up with on the way to collect her.

Flint would live—for now.

With all of the women moved into their new flats, he was going to be the patsy.

Chapter Twenty-One

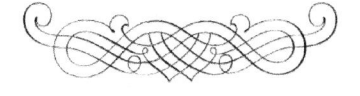

Margo had suffered greatly by keeping the secret. She didn't sleep much these days, barely ate, and she jumped at every little thing. A bag of nerves, that's what Mum had called her. She'd also asked why, but Margo had been unable to provide an adequate answer. It was becoming a bit easier to maintain a façade, but her husband, Julian, had mentioned last

time he was home that she didn't seem the same. Yes, the money had helped take away some of the sting being skint had brought, but sometimes she didn't think it was worth the worry she'd carried with her as a latent passenger for the past six months. She'd lost weight, which wasn't a bad thing in her eyes as she'd put it on after having the children, but she'd much rather not look so gaunt. Dark shadows lived under her eyes, and Julian had asked whether she needed to visit the doctor — "Are you ill, love?"

No, she wasn't ill, just riddled with guilt and fear; it ate away at her, and unless she kept herself busy, it swirled around her head until she threw up. Every day she entertained the scenario that the police would come to her door, maybe Quenton getting an attack of conscience and confessing to setting up the robbery and telling Nora to kill those boys. But according to the papers, he was having a great time, attending parties in London and gadding about abroad. People gossiped about how disgusting it was for him to behave like that, and so soon after his wife and kids had died, too. Goosemoor Senior and his wife had snuffed it an' all, the local rag stating they'd died from broken hearts. Sensationalism at its best.

They would have been broken even more had the couple known their son had brought everything about.

Or should that be the mysterious man who'd sent him the letter? Margo would like to brain him. He'd set off a sequence of terrible events, and everyone involved was now paying for it while he probably enjoyed the five thousand pounds without a thought to who'd ensured the money had reached his grubby hands.

Had he forced Quenton to tell Nora to kill his wife and boys? Was that too far-fetched an assumption? Margo entertained whether Quenton had tricked them—there was no man who'd written a letter, Quenton had written it himself, putting it in the drawer for Nora to find, knowing she'd be organising his dressing room that day. He'd then funded his holidays with the five grand, continuing his lavish existence afterwards with life insurance money and the payout for the jewellery. He'd **wanted** *his wife and kids killed, that much was startlingly obvious, and she wouldn't be swayed regarding her thoughts on the matter.*

They'd been conned. Nora wouldn't have it, though. She believed Quenton had told her the truth about the blackmail. Whatever, they'd never agree on certain things now, ever. Mainly those boys' bodies, dead on the carpet. Nora's excuse for obeying Quenton didn't hold water as far as Margo was concerned. She'd even dabbled with the idea that Quenton and

Nora were in on this together, going so far as to imagine them having an affair. Darcy had found out, and they'd had to get rid of her. Margo had been waiting for Nora to announce she'd suddenly fallen in love with the lord and was moving in with him, then that would confirm her suspicions.

Was that why Oscar had been shot in the head? She hadn't exactly been cut up after the police had gone that night. She'd been more interested in shoving cider down her neck.

Oh God, pack it in. Nora wouldn't do anything like that.

She talked herself out of those scenarios regularly, only for them to keep returning. She had nightmares at least once a week, watching those boys getting shot every time, waking up sweating and crying. Julian spent a lot of time away from home—he was in the army—so at least he didn't know how often she had bad dreams. She'd hidden her cash in a wicker shopping bag in the coal shed, popping some in the bank every now and then. She'd bought a small shop for cash, no questions asked, and had built up her customer base. Julian and anyone else who'd enquired thought she rented the place.

But her new stream of income had been purchased with blood money. What should be a happy time because she wasn't burdened by debt or the cost of living was tainted. They'd all done well for themselves, changing their lives: Nora had bought her house and another her landlord had owned; Edie now ran a market stall, buying and selling clothes bought from snobs who'd got bored of their outfits; Lucia was still a cook at the school, but she'd upped her weekly food budget and made out she'd had a win on the pools so she could buy Barry a new car. They all met once a month round Nora's, the conversation always ending up on the robbery, how they felt about it, how they could move forward without feeling so bad.

If Margo had known the result of going into that manor in a balaclava would mean she'd be so unhappy, she'd never have agreed to do it. She should have backed out when she'd got the jitters in the car.

The one thing she hadn't bought yet was a newer model car; Barry's was so gorgeous she'd been thinking about getting the same one for a while. Now her shop was doing so well she could get one on hire purchase without anyone thinking anything of it. That was her job for today, a visit to the showroom. She'd left the shop in the capable hands of her sister who helped to run it, opting to walk as it wasn't that far and she could do with the fresh air. And it was *fresh, bloody cold, in fact. December had crept up quickly, and with her fancy coat wrapped around her, she trotted along, although she had to watch where she was going because of the frost and fog.*

She'd made it halfway down the busy high street before she got the sensation she was being watched. This had happened a lot lately, her standing behind the counter in her shop, convinced someone was out there looking in. A glance over her shoulder revealed no one who seemed sinister, or who resembled a copper, but what about those beyond the foggy veil? She put it down to paranoia that the police had her under observation and walked past a van delivering goods to the little supermarket. Another had parked behind it.

Someone jostled her on the left, sending her across the pavement and down the kerb between the vans. She stumbled forward, stopping just before she got to the open road. She went to turn and give whoever it was what for, but a shove to her back sent her careening forward. Her heartbeat escalated, pure fear and adrenaline entering her system, instinct telling her to run forward rather than go back towards whoever had pushed her. She checked right—a car came hurtling out of the fog, too fast when there were so many pedestrians around, and for a moment she froze. At the point her brain told her to dart across, the car came too close for her to escape it. It whacked into the side of her leg, sending her flying. She landed on the bonnet, sliding off onto the opposite side of the road and landing hard. Screams and shouts of alarm rang out, and despite the pain in her hip, she tried to stand. Glanced to her left.

Another car, this one also going too fast, looming out of the misty swirls. The front grille bore down on her, and at the moment of impact on her face, her head whacking onto the ground, she registered that the vehicle was going to go over her, that agony spread over her cheeks and forehead, that her nose was broken. Time slowed, and the pain of the wheels crunching her arm bones pushed out the last scream she'd ever release.

Nora paused at the sound of her name being called across the factory floor. She peered over at where it had come from. She'd just about heard it above the clatter of the machines. Cheryl beckoned her and led her into the room on the other side of reception where she worked. Fuck, were the police here? Had they finally come to arrest her?

"What's the matter?" Nora's heart would give out on her one of these days.

"Someone called Lucia's on the blower. She says it's important. We don't normally allow staff to get personal calls, as you know, but she honestly sounds frantic. I thought it best to come and get you. I won't tell the boss if you won't."

Oh God…

Cheryl opened the door to reception and held it wide. "I'll leave you to it for a minute."

Nora dipped past her, sick to her stomach, the door closing behind her. What had happened? For Lucia to phone her at work, it had to be bad, didn't it? Nora went to the desk and picked up the receiver lying on the desk.

"Hello?"

"Nora?"

"Yes…"

"It's Margo."

"No it isn't, it's Lucia."

"Yes, it's me, but I meant it's about *Margo."*

"Fucking hell. Has she gone and opened her mouth or something? I knew she was finding this difficult, but for God's sake, it's not just her getting in the shit here, is it. I had a feeling she'd buckle."

"It's nothing like that. The headmistress came to find me in the kitchen. The police had been to the

school, and they asked me if I could take Margo's kids to mine because they know we're mates."

"Why? What's gone on?"

"She's been knocked over."

Nora shook her head. Was it wicked to be relieved Margo was just hurt and she hadn't gone blabbing to the police? "Bloody hell, where was this?"

"She was walking down the high street and stumbled down a kerb. She went to cross the road and got mowed down. But that's not the worst of it."

"Tell me…"

"She tried to get up, and another car came and ran over her. She died on the road. People tried to save her, but she wouldn't wake up. The impact was…well, you can imagine."

Nora staggered around the desk to sit. She couldn't breathe properly, her lungs tight, her head full of images of a crushed and flattened Margo. All that blood. It was so foggy today, so had anyone actually seen what had happened? They must have if they knew she'd gone down the kerb. "That poor cow…"

"I know. Her kids are in bits; I've got them colouring in at the kitchen table to try and keep their minds off it until Margo's mum comes to get them. The police got hold of Julian wherever he is, and he's been

given leave to come home. I can't...I mean, what a fucking horrible way to go."

"Have you told Edie?"

"I'm just about to do that now. I'll have to ring the pub and get someone to go out to her stall."

Chuffed at being phoned first, Nora then squashed that feeling. It wasn't appropriate. "We can pool some money to help with the funeral, tell Julian we did a whip-round or something to cover for how we can afford it."

"Yeah, and pay for the flowers and whatnot. We'll sort the food for the wake, save him worrying. It hasn't sunk in yet that we'll never see her again. I'm trying to keep it together for the children. I was going to phone Barry after I've let Edie know. I don't want to cope with this on my own."

"I can come round, don't bother Barry when he's at work. I'll ask if I can leave now. I do enough overtime at short notice, so it should be okay."

"Thanks. See you in a bit."

Nora put the phone in the cradle and closed her eyes, hot tears leaking. To anyone observing, Margo had really got her shit together the past six months; it was only the four of them who knew how much she'd struggled behind the façade. Her shop was doing so well, the perfect disguise for her spending more money than usual. Julian would be devastated, he adored her. What were the odds of this happening, eh? Had she been distracted and that's why she went down the kerb? The high street would be extra busy today; it was Friday, and there was the market just round the corner in the courtyard. Had it been too packed and foggy for anyone to see clearly? And why were drivers going so fast in this weather?

Nora opened her eyes and jumped.

Cheryl stood there. "Everything all right?"

Nora swiped her eyes with the back of her hand. "My friend's been run over and killed."

"Oh. Shit."

"I need to go and help look after her kids. Their dad's in the army somewhere abroad, so it'll be a while before he's back."

"Go," Cheryl said. "I'll explain it to the boss."

"Thanks."

Nora went to the staffroom to collect her handbag from her locker. She left the factory and contemplated going to see if Ron was in The Eagle so she could get a lift to Lucia's. She usually got the bus to work. But he might ask for another favour, and she couldn't handle that, not today. Luckily, a cab trundled towards her, so she flagged it down. All the way to Lucia's she tried to get to grips with Margo being dead. It didn't seem possible that the once vibrant, funny, often arsey woman was no longer with them. How sad that the last six months of her life had been blighted by guilt. Her laughter hadn't been so lively, the sparkles in her eyes non-existent. The robbery had dulled her shine, and now it was snuffed out completely.

Fate had blown out her candle.

And it was Oscar's fault.

Nora paid the cabbie and got out, taking a deep breath as she walked up the garden path. The door flew open, and Lucia shot out, grabbing Nora in a hug and crying on her shoulder. Seeing Nora must have flicked an emotional switch.

Nora stepped back and held her friend's upper arms. "Are you okay?"

"No."

"Sorry, that was a stupid question. You told Edie?"

Lucia nodded. "She's packing up the stall, dropping her gear off at the lock-up and coming round."

"How are the kids?"

"One kept crying, but the other was in shock. Margo's mum's just left with them. I sound nasty, but thank God they've gone. I mean, how the hell do you comfort little kids when their mum's dead?"

"I wouldn't know," Nora said bitterly. *"I pulled the trigger before I could even think about comforting those boys."*

"Jesus, Nora, keep your voice own."

Selfish of her—what was new these days?—Nora relaxed now she wouldn't have to try and be nice to Margo's kids. She wasn't in the best frame of mind to deal with blubbering nippers and needed a stiff drink.

In the house, they sat round the kitchen table with whiskey in their tea.

"I suppose her sister will carry on with the shop," Lucia said. *"What the hell is Julian going to think when he finds some of the money in the coal shed?"*

"Maybe he'll assume they're takings."

"What, thousands of pounds? And why would she have put it in the shed? There's still too much there for him to think that."

Nora shrugged. "We can't tell him where it was from."

"I know that, I'm not daft."

"He'll likely keep it quiet. Wouldn't you?"

Lucia nodded. "Too right."

"Perhaps we should go round there and get it."

"Sod off!"

They sat in silence until the doorbell rang. Lucia got up to answer it, returning with Edie in tow. Edie sat,

Lucia finding another cup and pouring tea from the pot, adding booze.

She lowered onto her chair. "Did you hear anything in town before you left?"

Edie nodded. "Albert on the stall next to mine nipped to the café just before the accident happened. He gave me the gossip. One person who was right behind her said she was pushed into the road between two delivery vans by some bearded bloke in a flat cap, but you know what people are like in the high street on a Friday. Everyone shoves to get through the crowds. It was likely an accident with fucking horrible consequences."

"But what if she was pushed on purpose?" Nora asked.

"Who'd do that to her, though?" Edie asked.

"Fuck knows," Lucia said. "She didn't have any enemies, wasn't the type."

An uneasy feeling settled inside Nora, but she didn't voice her concern. It was stupid to think Quenton had arranged for Margo to be killed. Wasn't it?

Chapter Twenty-Two

Flint had shit himself when the twins had turned up late last night. He'd convinced himself Anaisha had snooped on his laptop and she'd seen the chat box, told them what she'd discovered. He'd been so good, staying away from London Teens, not buying a new perv laptop, but the pull to return had finally got hold of him. He'd always likened his grooming ways to a drug, and him giving in to it just proved that some addictions couldn't be broken, even when you knew you could end up either going to prison or being killed by The Brothers.

But they hadn't come round about the laptop. He wasn't too happy about the job he'd been given. He supposed it made sense—he wasn't about to tell anyone what he had to do this sunny Sunday morning, was he, whereas if someone else had been chosen they might well have spilled details of it before the men had even been killed, a bit of bragging to their mates that they'd been entrusted with the mission to off a few blokes.

It just happened to be Flint's weekend off, and he'd been bored yesterday, the prickly kind of tedium where nothing took his mind off talking to young girls. He'd annoyed himself for succumbing while at the same time excited to be jumping back in. Best_Girl was the type to give up a picture pretty quickly, he'd sensed that, and he'd been right. Having to wait until Anaisha had gone to take a look at it had done his tree in, but it was a beauty. He'd get a fair amount of customers wanting to buy it.

The panic that had rippled through him when the doorbell had pealed last night had him snapping the laptop shut. And thank God he had, because George and Greg had stood at his front door and insisted on coming in. They hadn't told him when he had to do the killing spree until they'd messaged him early this morning, telling him to get his arse in gear and meet them in the Noodle car park.

In their taxi, gloves on, George had handed over a balaclava still in its sealed packet, an unregistered gun from their stash, ammunition, plus another burner phone that would be destroyed afterwards by the twins. Flint had to wear black, move around as though he was well used to using a gun, and generally lead any witnesses down the path of believing he was someone to be afraid of. That way, any do-gooders would think twice about trying to stop him.

He'd returned to his flat and got his dark clothes on. Stuck ammo in his coat pocket. It wasn't just him out in the field today. Diddy and Kaiser, among others, were keeping watch on the targets, one each. Everyone had a new burner for the operation, which made complete sense.

Flint glanced at the clock. Ten a.m.

He checked WhatsApp on the burner for updates and to refresh his memory on what the targets looked like. All of their photos had been uploaded, and he studied each face, familiarising himself with their features.

Balaclava in the other pocket, the gun in a holster beneath his coat, he popped gloves on and left the flat. In a stolen car left at the kerb by Dwyane, he headed towards the home of Abuser 1. Apparently, A1 had yet to open his bedroom curtains and had been on a bender last night, arriving home with a bird who'd crept out around three in the morning to do the walk of shame. A1 would be tired, disorientated when Flint noisily drew him outside. The neighbours had to get an eye and earful of what was going on—the aim was to convince them a soldier with PTSD had lost the plot so the police were sent in the wrong direction of who the perpetrator was.

Once he'd messaged the group chat with the signal 'A1 COMPLETE', he had to move quickly to the next available target, picking off the easier ones first. The others were all out and about, so they'd appear more like random kills.

He arrived in A1's street, tugged the balaclava on, and got out of the car, leaving the engine running and the driver's door ajar. From a front garden, he snatched up a rock from the border display, then went back out onto the pavement to create a scene.

"Who the fuck wants a fight?" he shouted. "Who the bloody fuck wants to take me down? Come on! Someone must have the balls." He took the gun out and waved it around. "Let's be having you!"

He kept going, heads poking around curtains. Someone drove down the street, indicating as if to park, then clapped eyes on the gun and kept going. Flint ranted on, more faces appearing behind the panes, and, at last, A1's.

Flint threw the rock at his bedroom window. It bounced off. "What are you staring at, eh? Come and have a go if you think you're hard enough!"

A1 opened the window wide and stuck his face out. "What the fuck's your problem? Hiding behind a mask? Fucking coward."

Flint raised the gun and fired, hitting A1 in the forehead—the desired spot for every one of them. He legged it to the car, getting in and zooming off. He passed a man sitting in a work van—was he one of the twins' fellas?

Two streets away, he pulled over.

F: A1 COMPLETE.

He checked the updates. A2 stood in a queue at a breakfast food van outside a pub. Shit, a queue—too dangerous for the other people, but Flint may well have to kill him there anyway if the bloke didn't move on in time. A3 was having a coffee and eating something in his blue Mini in the nearby Tesco car park, so he'd do. Flint went there, driving up and down the aisles between cars. A bloke with a beard stood beside the cashpoint machines and nodded. Flint nodded back and drove by, looking for the Mini. He spotted it, came to a stop in front of it to block the bloke in, and got out. He jerked the gun in the air as an indication for A3 to leave his car. Instead, the man started his engine and reversed into the car behind, desperately trying to shove it backwards.

Flint fired a shot through the windscreen, hitting him right between the eyes.

He jumped in the stolen car again and sped towards the exit. Some old dodger pushing a full trolley walked along slowly, preventing Flint from leaving. He tooted the horn, opened the window, and shot the fucker in the shin. He hadn't been given permission to add casualties to the list, but it would look more authentic now. He'd get a right bollocking for it, but he'd explain his thinking, calm the twins down.

He gunned it, checking the rearview. Shoppers, also with trolleys, rushed to help the fallen bloke, and someone chased after *his* trolley which rolled away.

Flint made it to a side street.

F: A3 COMPLETE.

More updates. A2 had now left the van queue and sat at one of the nearby wooden tables outside the pub, away from people, although two other tables were occupied. Flint steeled himself to get there as quickly as possible. By now, the police would know something was going down as the neighbours in A1's street would have been on the blower, and it'd be panic stations once news spread from Tesco.

He made it to the pub in short time and assessed his surroundings, doing a drive-by. The queue, eight people in it. Two workers inside the food van. A man and woman eating sausage baguettes at one table; a couple of teenagers at another; and A2 wolfing down a bacon sandwich, steam from his polystyrene cup rising.

U-turn completed, Flint drove back towards A2. He lowered the window, shouted a few obscenities and claimed God and Jesus were bastards, then fired. The force of the bullet flung A2 backwards, off the seat and onto the ground. The teenagers shrieked and ran off, but the older couple froze. Flint was of a mind to create another casualty with a superficial flesh wound, but with the queue scattering, someone likely videoing him on their phone, and the shutters coming down on the food van, plus he wasn't sure which person watching worked for the twins, he didn't have a steady enough target.

"It's your lucky day, fuckers!" he shouted out of the window and drove away.

Adrenaline kept him going, but if there was too much of a gap between A2 and A4, he'd soon be tired, his energy depleted. He swung the car into another side street behind a Transit and got the burner out.

F: A2 COMPLETE.

He read the updates: the police had arrived at A1's street and at Tesco. Mayhem, apparently. A4 had been smoking outside a bookies with a mate for the past five minutes. Flint drove there, parked at a haphazard angle outside, but no one smoked any fags. Shoppers dispersed quickly when he darted out of the car, the balaclava and gun likely shitting them up.

He glanced at the phone—A4 had gone inside Betty's Bets.

Fuck.

Flint lunged across the pavement and entered the bookies. Customers jumped upon seeing him, and someone behind the plastic-enclosed counter reached downwards, probably to press a panic button. Lucky for Flint, he'd wedged the door open with his heel so any locking mechanism couldn't trap him inside. Men backed away towards a door marked STAFF, and Flint copped an eyeful of A4.

Gun lifted, he shouted, "Who's it to be, eh? Which one of you fuckers is going to Hell with me?" He pulled the trigger, the bullet once again penetrating a forehead.

Except it wasn't A4's.

Shit. Bollocks.

The innocent man dropped to the floor, revealing A4 who'd crouched and darted behind him just at the right time. But now he was exposed, on his haunches, so Flint tugged at the trigger again. A4 keeled over on top of the dead bloke, and Flint ranted about the Devil for good measure, then sprinted to the car, shoppers screaming and darting out of his way in fear.

He pegged it to the agreed location where another stolen car awaited him in a road with a park on the right and the backs of houses on the left. He found the keys on the front wheel arch and got in, snatched the balaclava off, and counted the people in the park. No adults, just four kids, and they weren't paying any attention to him, too busy on the swings and a roundabout. He got going. Passed the houses and gave them the once-over, thankful no one stood at their top windows.

The dopamine rush from a successful mission careened through him, and he whooped, slapping the steering wheel. He raced to the meeting spot where George and Greg waited for him in their van, forensic suits on, fake beards and gloves. It wasn't until he'd got in the back that the fear hit him regarding what they were going to say when they found out he'd shot the old man and that bloke. Was that why they were in the white suits? Were they going to kill him for disobeying them? They must know already because they were in the chat group.

"You got them all," Greg said and eased away from the kerb.

"Yep."

George turned his head to look over at Flint. "You hit an old boy at Tesco."

"He wouldn't get out of the fucking way and was blocking the exit. There was no other place for me to get out."

"Your first question should have been: I didn't kill him, did I?"

"Sorry. Did I?"

"No, but you did kill the one in the bookies. We know what happened because one of our men was in there at the time, so we'll let you off—that wasn't your fault."

"Thank fuck for that. The target snuck behind him just as I fired."

Greg *hmmed*.

George elbowed him. "Right, let's get Flint to the warehouse so he can get those clothes off, have a shower, and change into a tracksuit."

Flint rested against the side of the van and closed his eyes. Shit, he was tired.

Chapter Twenty-Three

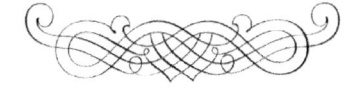

MALE, 36, SEEKS WOMAN, 30-40,
FOR MEANINGFUL RELATIONSHIP
WITH A VIEW TO MARRIAGE AND
CHILDREN. DOG LOVER A MUST.
DARK HAIR PREFERRED.
SERIOUS APPLICANTS ONLY.

Edie was on her way to a blind date. Albert, who ran the antiques stall beside hers, had pointed out an ad in the local paper in the Lonely Hearts section. He reckoned it was about time she got herself a new man. He'd been most insistent, saying it wouldn't do any harm, and who knew, she might just meet the love of her life.

"Stranger things have happened. Life's too short not to take some chances," he'd said. "Look what happened to your mate, Margo. You might not be here this time tomorrow. Nothing is promised."

Excitement had swirled through her when she'd phoned the number at the bottom of the ad, her breath catching at the sound of the man's deep voice. He'd sounded nice, nothing like her husband who'd left her shortly after the robbery, saying her alcohol intake had increased too much for his liking and she was no longer the woman he'd married. She couldn't argue with that. She'd taken her anxiety out on him, and he'd stopped staying in at night, preferring to go out instead. Their divorce was imminent. Turned out he'd been seeing some slag down the road for months and had used Edie's new affair with drink as an excuse to leave.

Bastard.

She'd been on a few nights out since Margo's death, dragging her next-door neighbour with her as Lucia and Nora hadn't wanted to go. They'd taken Margo's passing hard. Edie had, too, but her way of dealing with it—or not *dealing with it—was to party hard after work and pretend it hadn't happened. Hardly healthy for her body or her mind, but she'd found during the aftermath of the robbery and witnessing Nora shooting three people that tuning it out was the only way she coped. With her recent dumping added to the mix, she really had too much to deal with. Alcohol took away real life and exchanged it for sunshine and rainbows, laughter and fun.*

On the bright side, her market stall was doing well, and life was good if she didn't count the bad dreams and the guilt that poked at her. It didn't help that they rehashed the robbery every time they got together for drinks at Nora's, reminding themselves every month that they were bad people, Nora trying to make them feel better by saying she was the worst. Tack onto that introspection about Margo's death that tended to crop up, and Edie was beginning to think that maybe they should abandon their gatherings and go their separate ways. They weren't moving on if they continued to pick the events apart.

She stood on the street opposite the small parade of shops on her housing estate, Christmas decorations still sparkling in windows even though New Year had come and gone. A light drizzle fell, settling on her face. She paused at the kerb, looking both ways, and hated that doing something that used to be so simple was accompanied by a voice inside, warning her to be extra careful: "Don't end up like Margo, don't end up like Margo…"

She crossed over, going down past the parade into the next street where the pub stood, entering and searching for a man with a red hanky in the front pocket of his suit jacket; he'd told her to look out for that. He stood at the bar already facing her—he'd turned to see who'd come in—and a big smile lit up his face. Dark-brown hair, a little wavy. A moustache sat beneath a blunt-ended Roman nose, his hazel eyes such an unusual shade she knew she'd seen them before. They were the type you'd never forget.

"You're the man who spoke to Albert for ages last week, aren't you?" She hung her handbag strap at the crook of her elbow. "Sorry for blurting that out. I'm Edie."

"Ted. And yes, I spoke to Albert."

"Do you like antiques, then?"

"I'm a collector, hence the chat we had. What would you like to drink?"

"Vodka and tonic, please."

Ted ordered that for her and another for himself, a pint of beer. They moved to a table in the corner, away from the rowdier customers, and dived into conversation. It was nice to have a date with someone more refined. Ted wasn't as cultured as Quenton, but he wasn't a rough type from the East End either. They nattered for a couple of hours as well as having pie and mash for dinner. Six or seven vodkas later, everything paid for by Ted, and Edie had convinced herself he was 'the one' and that they should go back to her place.

They left the pub arm in arm, and she got the cabbie to drop them at the end of the street next to hers. She led him down an alley at the back of her place—she didn't want the neighbours seeing her with a bloke just yet. Too many questions, and for some reason, she didn't want her ex knowing her business. He'd moved in with the slag, rubbing salt in the wound as the house was only four doors down.

They picked their way through the back garden and entered the house, Edie decidedly squiffy. She locked the door, turning to find Ted standing there staring at her oddly. Had he drunk too much and he felt off, too? No, he'd only had two and a half pints.

"What's the matter?" she asked.

He blinked. "Oh, nothing."

"Do you want a nightcap or a coffee?"

*"I'll make it. You go and get comfortable in bed."
He winked.*

Edie giggled and rushed upstairs, going into the bathroom for a quick wee and to freshen up. She changed out of her dress into a pretty lace-edged black nightie and got into bed, her excitement levels rising as well as a dash of anxiety.

She hadn't slept with anyone since her husband had fucked off. What if Ted didn't like her body or the shape of her tits? What if he didn't like the way she kissed?

More than tipsy from the vodka, her head spinning, she rested against the headboard and closed her eyes. The tug of sleep yanked at her quickly, and she jolted herself awake, but her eyes were so heavy she couldn't keep them open.

On the second date, she'd only have two vodkas.

The next time she woke, her bedroom door was shut and the distinct smell of smoke had her shooting out of bed. She tried to get out, but the handle was hot and burned her palm. Panicked, she grabbed her dress and wrapped it around the handle, pulling on it. The door was stuck. A rumbling noise then the pop of glass shattering increased the panic—was the house on fire? And where was Ted? Was he trapped, too? She dashed over to the window, then remembered the frame had been painted so much it no longer opened. It didn't have a large pane, rather eight small ones, and she wouldn't be able to climb through any of them.

Regardless, she looked around for something to smash them with, something hard enough that would break the framework around each sheet of glass, but other than a hairbrush, there was nothing. So she whacked on them with the sides of her fists, screaming and shouting for help. She coughed, the smoke tickling the back of her throat.

A couple of neighbours opposite ran out of their houses, staring at hers, their mouths dropping open. One of them ran back inside, hopefully to ring the fire brigade, and the other stepped closer, dithering as though undecided on what she should do. More people joined her, a crowd gathering, all of them gawping up at her but not doing anything.

The fire must be too far gone, and the nasty realisation hit her in the chest that no one was prepared to help her, or they couldn't because there was no way they could get inside and upstairs without getting burnt. She sobbed against the glass, coughing, and turned to look at the door. Smoke chuntered in beneath it, and the loud crackle of fire eating the wood told her she was going to die in here. The smoke would send her to sleep before the flames could lick her all over, but still, the fear of that, of her life ending, sent a shot of pure adrenaline through her.

Shaking, she faced the window and hit the glass harder, hammering and hammering until the small pane cracked. A punch to its centre sent shards outwards, her arm going through and getting cut. She pulled it back through and screamed into the hole she'd created, a useless plea, and from the corner of her eye spotted the insidious smoke had crept in even more, reaching waist height, black billows of it.

Coughing again, unable to stop now she'd started, Edie stuck her face to the hole so she could breathe fresh air. Then a new surge of wanting to live took over, and she hit at another pane. If she could break it, the thin wooden strut of frame in between might snap if she smacked at it. She'd have to repeat it again with a third pane and a second strut to create a big enough opening, but what else could she do?

She broke another pane, but the strut wouldn't budge. The smoke rose, and she swore she was being cooked by the heat coming through the door from the landing. Her head lightened, and she coughed, inhaling smoke then coughing even more. She grabbed her dress to put it over her mouth, dropping to the floor where the smoke had dissipated as it climbed upwards into the air, it's destination the holes in the window.

She didn't remember anything else.

Albert sat beside the radio in his living room and thought about Edie going on her date tonight with that Ted fella. Nice chap. Albert was pleased with himself for helping him out by telling Edie about that lonely hearts advert in the paper. Ted had told Albert he'd taken a fancy to Edie last week and didn't have the courage to ask her out to her face, so he'd come up with the idea of the ad. Albert had agreed to point it out to her when it appeared, and that was that, Bob's your uncle.

It was closing in on half eleven, so he'd wait for this song to finish then trot off upstairs. The sound of a siren had him getting up to part the curtains and look outside. A fire engine barrelled past. Sending up a prayer for whoever needed help, he went into the hallway and opened the front door. Glanced up and down the street. The engine had gone, and there was no fire that he could see, so he returned indoors and locked up.

Bedtime.

A man in a suit with a red hanky in his pocket stood with the neighbours out the front of Edie's house. The fire engine rumbled, men in uniform battling the flames. Ted, as he'd called himself for this job, couldn't wait to get the wig and moustache off, go home and wash the night's work off him, but he lingered to find out whether his task had been completed.

He'd get paid tomorrow by a middleman. Whoever wanted Edie killed had been specific about the method. Ted had been told to jam a wooden wedge under her bedroom door so she couldn't get out. Seemed it had worked, even though the door opened inwards. And the date idea had been genius, as had the ad in the paper. Shame he'd had to deceive Albert, though. Still, a payday was a payday, wasn't it, and he shouldn't care who he had to use in order to do what he'd been asked to do.

A shout went up, and the neighbours all talked at once. Their words filtered to him: "Couldn't get her out in time…" and "She's gone, poor cow."

Ted smiled and walked away.

Killing the other two had failed so far, but he wasn't the type to give up so long as money was on the table.

Nora had stayed behind for a lock-in at the Cock and Hen on her estate. Edie had gone out on a date, and Lucia hadn't felt like going to the pub. Three sheets to the wind, Nora weaved her way towards home. She'd take the chance and use the shortcut through the park so veered down the alley that led to it.

Footsteps from behind had her spinning to check who was there. She was on edge lately, what with almost being knocked over—a bit too much of a coincidence if you asked her, plus that electric shock she'd had at the factory. Then there was that man who'd broken into Lucia's, Barry scaring him off with the cricket bat. She was convinced someone was trying to kill them, like they'd killed Margo.

A shape darker than the night whacked into her, and she stumbled and fell to her knees. Her instincts screamed for her to run, so she got to her feet, but he was on her, grabbing her arm and marching her towards the park.

"Oi, what's your game?" a man shouted from the blackness ahead. "Are you all right, love?"

"He's… Help! I don't know him. He pushed me…"

The bloke holding her let go, called her an annoying bitch, and ran back towards the street behind. The newcomer chased after him, and Nora legged it across the park, her handbag slapping against her side, the night seeming to close in on her, her attention on the distant glow of the lampposts glistening from the other side of the trees.

Had Ron sent someone to...to what, hurt her? Had someone else used the gun before her and it had been tied to the robbery? Was she supposed to be punished for that? Or was that bloke just a random chancer, a rapist? Or was this to do with Quenton?

Throat drying out from her rapid breathing, she launched herself into a cut-through that led to a residential street and sprinted until she reached hers. She took her keys out of her bag as she ran, out of breath and crying by the time she got to her house. She contemplated knocking on Roger's door just so she had someone with her but instead flung herself inside and slammed the door. Hand shaking, she drew the top and bottom bolts across, one of them sticking, frustrating the hell out of her. It finally slid into place, and she leaned on the wall beside the door to calm herself down.

The trilling of the phone had her screeching, and she snatched it up. "Hello?"

"It's me."

"Oh God, Lucia, some bloke just tried...I don't know what *he was going to do, but he pushed me to the ground in an alley by the park and this other man*

came and went after him. I could have been raped! Fucking hell…"

"Are you okay?"

"Would you be?"

"Sorry."

"I can't stop shaking."

"Do you want me to come round?"

Nora sagged with relief. "Yes. Can you stay the night? I'm shit-scared of being on my own."

"Yeah, Barry won't mind. You know what he's like, anything to please me."

Nora had always been jealous of that, seeing as Oscar had done anything to upset her. Then the time dawned on her. A phone call this late couldn't be good news. "Why did you ring me?"

"It'll keep. I'll tell you when I get there. It's better done in person anyway."

"You're scaring me."

"Go and make a cuppa or something, I won't be long."

The wait for Lucia full of tension, Nora paced her hallway, fuck making tea. The flash of headlights scarfed through the glass of the front door a few minutes later. She dipped into the living room to check out of the window, making sure it was Lucia, then undid the bolts. Lucia got out of the car and came towards the house. Barry drove off, giving a wave. He appeared worried about something, sad. Lucia must have told him about the potential rapist.

Nora swerved her attention to her friend. Lucia's face wasn't just showing her concern for what had happened to Nora. Something else was wrong. It had to be for Lucia to phone past nine o'clock. Nora retreated into the house and sat on the stairs, dreading whatever blow was coming her way. Their lives had been cursed since the robbery.

Lucia came in, locked up, and popped her overnight bag on the floor. "You're going to need some tissues."

Nora's heart sank. "Oh God, why?"

"Edie's dead, love."

Chapter Twenty-Four

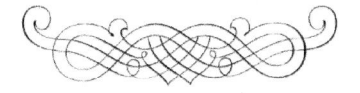

Flint didn't get to take his clothes off, have a shower, and change into a tracksuit. George gripped the back of the copper's hair as soon as they entered the warehouse and marched him to the wooden torture chair. He forced him to sit, Flint staring up at him with fear in his eyes. He probably thought George was arsey about the old man and the fella in the bookies, but he'd soon find out that wasn't the case.

"Fishy_For_Life. It's you, isn't it."

Flint didn't hide his expression of shock in time. "What? It was Kendall, you *know* that."

"No, you wanted us to *think* it was Kendall, but it wasn't. He *did* say Fishy wasn't him right up until he confessed under pressure. A bit like crims must do at the station. They agree to anything just so the interrogation stops."

"Why the hell would I be Fishy? I'm not a perv!"

"Oh, but you are a perv, London_Lad."

Flint blinked, eyelashes fluttering far too much for an innocent man. "Eh?"

"The laptop. One of two we've left in your flat for your colleagues to find—but we have screenshots of the browser you didn't bother to shut down. Fuck, you didn't even bother putting in a passcode. Novice. One of our people typed a message to Best_Girl, telling her you're a bad man and you're sorry for asking for a picture. And you're messed up in the head and you'll fix it, make it all okay. And that you were Fishy. That killing spree's going to look like you went off your rocker with guilt, and when you're found with a bullet hole in your temple, case closed."

"Please, I can explain…"

"No amount of explaining can make this right. If I didn't need your body to be found because of the spree, I'd get Terry here, let him deal with you." George's anger crept to a new level. "You lied to us. You made out you felt sorry for Terry and his missus, acted like you wanted to find the scum who'd made their kid kill herself, but all along it was you." George paced, desperate to beat the shit out of him, but he couldn't. Any bruising would fuck things up. The only mark Flint could have on him was a bullet hole. "What did you do with the photos?"

"I'm not an actual paedo, I didn't download them so I could do dirty shit while looking at them. They were an income stream, that was all."

"Pardon?"

"I sold them online."

"What?"

"I made money out of them."

"I gathered that, sunshine, but what I'm having trouble with is the fact you're acting like it's no big deal to have chatted young girls up, got them to send you rude pictures, then you scared the shit out of them by forcing them to put money in envelopes and leave them in bins. What were you doing, hanging around nearby, watching them do it? Is that what got you off, the control you had over them? I bet you shit yourself when Summer turned up dead, didn't you."

"It all went wrong. It wasn't supposed to happen like that."

"You're not right in the head. You're damaged, and you damaged all those girls an' all. Gave them nightmares for the rest of their lives. I can see it now, you asking for a tenner or twenty quid, knowing that was the only amounts they could get their hands on without bringing attention to themselves. Summer worked in the chip shop. She'd have given you her wages that she'd worked hard for. You utter fucking cunt."

George had to walk away before he belted him one. Greg went over to stand beside Flint, likely in case he had a mind to run, not that he'd get very far.

"I *knew* there was something off about you," George said. "That's why I asked Anaisha to get all buddy with you. I couldn't put my finger on it, but now I know, and let me tell you, that was the last thing I thought you'd have been involved in." He stared at Greg, unable to look at Flint or he'd do him some damage. "Put his balaclava on. I can't stand to see his face."

Greg took it out of Flint's pocket and rammed it on, then removed the gun from the holster. Flint made to get up, but Greg pushed him back down.

"I don't think so," Greg said, reaching back to put the gun in his hood.

George went over to the tool table and selected a strand of rope long enough to tie Flint's wrists together over the sleeves of his coat—he couldn't risk leaving any marks. He handed it to Greg and stood behind Flint, hands on his shoulders to keep him in place while his brother got on with roping the wanker up.

"About the county line," George said. "Something's been bugging me about that. Did you tip them off, get them to move their business elsewhere?"

Flint looked guilty.

"Thought so. You know what's got to happen," George said. "You've come to the end of your filthy road. As you can imagine, I'm dying to carve you up, give you pain, let you feel every slice of an axe, but you've got to take the rap for the spree. A shame, but that's the way it has to be, so now you're tied up, we'd best get going."

He went round the side of the chair and took hold of Flint's arm. Greg grabbed the other, and they carted him out to the van. Shoved him in the back. George got in with him, and Greg sat in the driver's seat.

"I'm so fucking sorry," Flint whined.

Greg drove off and looked in the rearview. "No you're not. You're only sorry you got caught."

Flint sobbed, and George pondered whether to have a go at Janine for recommending this piece of shit to them in the first place. She'd told them he was happy-go-lucky at work but that she'd sensed something about him that meant he'd be a good fit for the firm — that underneath that jolly façade lurked someone dodgy. She'd picked up on the badness inside him, but George would bet she wouldn't have thought it was *this* bad. Maybe Anaisha had already told her what she'd discovered on the laptop. Mind you, if she had, Janine would have been in touch by now.

Greg stopped in front of the stolen car Flint had used. Thankfully, no one was in the park, so while they had such an excellent window of opportunity, they'd get the job done now.

George dragged Flint out of the van and ordered him to sit in the driver's side of the car. Greg joined him, and George lifted the spree gun from his brother's suit hood and took the second gun Greg held out to him. He untied the rope around Flint's wrists and draped in over the crook of his arm.

"Give me the burner phone you used for the spree," George said. "We've already taken your other one out of your flat. We don't want us linked to you, do we."

Flint took it out of his pocket, handed it over, and stared up at them out of the open car door, the skin around his eyes pale against the black of the mask. His lashes, wet from crying, had clumped together where he'd had a pity party for one in the van. George failed to give a toss.

"Now then, my old son. I'm going to give you this gun, and you're being given the easy way out. No shame to face, no prison, nothing. I'm going to shut this door, and you're going to take that balaclava off and shoot yourself in the right temple. I'm going to stand here with my gun to make sure you do it. Don't even think about going for the left temple so the bullet goes through the window and into me—we always wear bulletproof bests now. Have you got anything to say for me to pass on to Terry and Willow?"

"I'm sorry. I'm so fucking sorry. I didn't mean for it to happen. Summer wasn't supposed to kill herself."

George gave him the spree gun. Closed the door. Aimed the other gun at Flint who snatched the mask off, raised his weapon, shut his eyes, and fired. The blast sent him lurching towards the passenger seat, blood spatter spraying, the far window speckled with it.

George glanced at the backs of the houses, then at the park.

No one.

His anger had no outlet, and that was dangerous, but there was no one to take it out on. They got in the van, no words spoken.

I mean, what is there to fucking say?

They'd dropped the van at home and changed out of their forensic suits, removing the beards then burning the rope. George had showered—it had felt like the filth inside Flint had seeped through the paedo's pores and swarmed all over George's skin. In their usual grey suits, white shirts, and red ties, they'd got in the BMW and drove to the Meeks' street. Parked outside the house.

As it was murder, Janine had messaged to sarcastically thank them for the amount of work she had to do regarding the spree—ON A FUCKING SUNDAY!—so George responded, putting off going to see Terry and Willow for a minute or two.

GG: YOU KNEW IT WAS GOING TO HAPPEN, SO STOP WHINGING.

J: I HAVEN'T GOT TIME TO CHAT SHIT WITH YOU, AS YOU WELL KNOW. WE'RE RUNNING ROUND LIKE BLUE-ARSED FLIES TRYING TO LOCATE THE SHOOTER.

GG: YOU'LL FIND HIM IN A CAR OPPOSITE THE PARK ON LOOP LANE. HAS ANAISHA GOT HOLD OF YOU?

J: ANOTHER ANON TIP THAT JUST HAPPENED TO COME TO ME? FUCK'S SAKE! WHAT HAVE I TOLD YOU ABOUT KEEP DOING THAT? AND NO, I HAVEN'T HEARD FROM HER.

GG: IT'S FLINT.

J: Who is, the spree killer?

GG: Yeah, and he was Fishy_For_Life.

J: Are you fucking me about?

GG: No, because I don't find crap like that funny. Go and see him. You'll find all you need to know on a laptop currently sitting on his coffee table. We're off to tell Terry, so delay going round there for as long as you can to let them know who the real Fishy is.

He stuck the phone in his pocket. "Best we get on with it, then. I just let Janine know about Flint."

"I saw." Greg sighed. "How d'you think Terry's going to take the news?"

"He'll be naffed off he killed the wrong bloke, I know that much. A part of me wants to leave him thinking Kendall was the right man, but it's going to come out that it's Flint. Janine will have to go round and tell them anyway."

They left the car and approached the house.

Terry must have seen them outside. He opened the door before they could knock. "Everything all right?"

"On one hand, yes, it's more than all right, on the other…" George stepped past him into the house. He caught sight of Willow in the kitchen so went in there.

At the cooker, bacon sizzling and spitting in a frying pan, she asked, "Has something happened?"

"You could say that." George sat at the table. "You might want to switch the hob off and come and sit down."

Greg and Terry entered. Once they were all around the table, George jumped straight in.

"Kendall Reynolds wasn't Fishy."

Terry paled. "You what?"

Willow's temper flared. "So who the fuck is it, then?"

"Was," George said. "We dealt with him. It was Flint."

Willow stared from George to Greg to her husband. "Your fucking *copper*?"

God, it sounded so bad. "I'm afraid so."

Terry gripped the sides of his hair. "What the fuck? I mean, a sodding plod? And how the hell did you find out?"

George explained about Anaisha's discovery on the laptop.

"Why hasn't Janine got hold of us already?" Terry barked. "We've got a right to have the police come round and say who they think groomed our kid."

"Because we've only just told her. There's more to this…"

"Tell me." Terry ran a hand over his face. "Just bloody tell me."

George launched into the story about the women at Haven, how the spree was the only way to get all the men killed in one go. Once they'd found out Flint was Fishy, there'd been no other option but to use him to do the job. "It'll look like he killed himself in the car. A little message has been left in the chat box on his laptop. It says he was Fishy. I'd have loved for you to get revenge and kill him, but as you can probably understand, we needed him to take the rap for the spree. But you can console yourself with the fact you still killed a bad man. Kendall being involved in grooming girls, kidnapping them…he deserved the death he had."

"Flint, though…" Terry shook his head. "He was nice to me. He had the fucking gall to act like he wasn't the one who made Summer do what she did. He lied to my face. I swear to God, if he wasn't dead, I'd rip him apart."

Willow wiped tears from her eyes and cheeks. "But it's over now, properly over. His name will be shit in the papers and on social media. The police will look like complete arseholes for having a paedo in the ranks."

"Some might not believe it's him," Greg said, "and you need to prepare yourselves for that. Apparently, he was all smiles and Mr Helpful at work, so it'll be hard for his colleagues to match that to the man who went off to kill people."

George was about to open his mouth and tell them Summer's pictures were more than likely sitting on hundreds of laptops, looked at by perverts on the daily, but he closed his lips. These two had been through enough, they didn't need to know—not yet anyway. It was bound to come out during the investigation, though, if Flint had used the same laptop to talk to Summer. He'd have a bank account, and payments would lead to people who'd purchased the images. For now, he'd leave them to digest this bit of news before more smacked them in their faces later down the line.

"Have you had breakfast?" Willow asked, rising.

She was doing that thing many women did, what their Mum had done in times of crisis—keeping busy to stop herself from thinking too deeply. George and Greg had eaten a fry-up in the Noodle while the spree had gone on, but at a nod from his brother, George gave her nod of his own.

"That'd be lovely if you're offering. Thank you."

She shot over to the cooker.

Terry got up to switch the kettle on. "Cheers for coming round, we appreciate it."

George smiled. "Stating the obvious, but you'll have to look shocked when Janine comes to deliver the news if she's got Colin with her."

Janine's DS had no clue what she got up to.

Terry took cups off a mug tree. "Yep."

"How have you two been doing?"

"We're getting there. Or we were. We thought Kendall was the man, so we'd kind of accepted that and tried to move on. Now we'll have to do it all over again. But we'll cope. Summer wouldn't want us moping about. I was meant to tell you—or ask, rather—can I have a week off in June? We'd like to go abroad. We plan to visit all the places Summer might have. You know, live her life for her."

"Yep, and that's a brilliant idea."

George let out a quiet sigh. These two had been broken several times over yet still had the courage to face the world in their daughter's stead. He admired them for that. Vic was a wonder, he'd helped them so much.

They ate breakfast, avoiding Flint as a subject, another coping mechanism for them, George reckoned. He knew all about that. He filled his days with Estate business so he didn't have to think about the past and their mother.

Food gone, they hung around for another twenty minutes to be polite, then said their goodbyes. He could do with checking the news for mention of Quenton going missing, then there was Nora to contact so they could drop Lucia to her, then Nora could take her to Haven as if they'd just got back from their little holiday. He fancied a roast dinner at the Noodle, too, after a nap this afternoon.

But life was never quiet, so he might not get those forty winks.

Chapter Twenty-Five

Nora often sat and thought about the past and how awful it had been. She was older and wiser, and to the outsider was a happy woman with no skeletons in her closet. She had a lot to be happy about, life was good, but the year of the robbery and the one afterwards would forever encroach on her peace of mind.

Twenty-odd years had limped by, yet whenever she saw Ron she still shuddered. He'd had two more favours after she'd given the gun back, yet he hadn't helped her again in order for her to owe him. She supposed he'd taken what he'd wanted just because he could.

Julian had found the money in the coal shed and moved up north. She sometimes wondered whether he was okay now, content with someone else, and that the children hadn't suffered too much with the loss of their mother. More and more recently, Nora was convinced Quenton had killed Margo and Edie, then tried to get rid of herself and Lucia, too. Lucia didn't want to entertain that scenario, perhaps too much trauma to add to what they were already coping with, and as more years had passed with no other incidents, Nora had tried to put it down to paranoia. But her gut instinct wouldn't leave her be. It wasn't like she could do anything about it anyway. Quenton would likely laugh in her face if she stormed up to the manor and confronted him.

So she kept it to herself, as well as all those secrets, and immersed herself in the street and becoming the one person everyone turned to if they had an issue. She had to do good to erase the bad. If she was helpful enough, kind enough, maybe, if there was a God, he'd forgive her.

She doubted it, though. She was more inclined to believe the Devil awaited her at the gates of Hell. As was only right. She didn't deserve to go anywhere else.

Chapter Twenty-Six

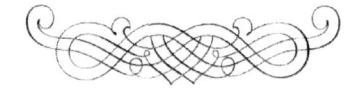

Nora had used the little tool kit and removed the jewels from their mounts earlier this morning. They didn't look as pretty this way, but she couldn't go to Essex and visit Pinocchio while they were still a part of the necklace-and-earring set. She'd stopped at a pay phone on the way back from Margate to ring the shop and check it was open today, what with it being Sunday. It was, so she'd driven to Essex and parked in a multistorey, so different to when she'd hopped off the bus the last time she'd come here. So, the pawnshop still existed. Whether Pinocchio still ran it was anyone's guess. She couldn't tell from the bloke's voice on the phone whether it was him or not.

The first time she'd been young, with bobbed black hair and severe eyebrows she'd thought had given her a unique look. Now, she was far too grey for her liking, and her eyebrows were no longer plucked, resembling bushy beetles, so would he even recognise her?

She pushed open the door, the same bell tinkling above it. An old man stood behind the counter, and it took her a moment to realise it was him. She'd remembered him as she'd last seen him, so this was a bit of a jolt. He glanced over at who'd entered and frowned, then his face lit up.

So he knew who she was, then.

"Ah, long time no see. So it was you on the blower earlier, was it?" He gestured to her. "Lock the door. I assume you've brought the ruby-and-diamond set. Took you long enough."

God, had he known all along that she'd kept them? That she was one of the robbers and not just a fence?

She approached him, dragging her emotional baggage with her, the load heavier than the previous time. She took the jewellery case out of her bag and placed it on the counter. "I did the best job I could in taking them out of the necklace and earrings."

"I hope you didn't bloody scratch them. You should have let me do it." He opened the box and, using what she now knew was a loupe, inspected the gems. "All right, I'll give it to you, you did a good job. Fuck me, these are worth a fortune. Bet you wish you'd brought them to me years ago."

"I was too scared to. You know they've been in the news."

"Yeah, as has their owner this morning. Did you hear?"

Startled, even though she'd known this would happen, she covered up her unease. "Heard what?"

"He was reported missing by his cleaner. She ran across to this other house on the grounds, and they rang the police."

The people at the Gables must have come back early. Fuck. What else have they told the coppers? Did they see anything last night?

"They never saw fuck all, in case you're wondering." Pinocchio took a notepad from beside the till and repeated his actions from the past, pushing it towards her so she could see the price he was offering.

"Blimey." The number fair took the wind from her sails. "I knew they were worth quite a bit, but not *that* much."

"We can't have a bank transfer going on, not for this lot, but I've actually got enough cash in the safe. I haven't banked the takings this week yet, and I've had a certain customer pay me a lot of dosh, if you catch my drift."

"Don't you worry you'll get robbed?"

"People round here wouldn't dare."

But you're old, an easy target, she wanted to say, then remembered she was old, too.

He put the case in the safe and took wads of money out. Counted it in front of her and, at her nod, he placed it in a couple of large manilla envelopes. At least she didn't have the worry of carrying it all on the bus. He creaked from behind the counter and ambled over to the window, pulling the blind. He did the same over the door and paused with his palm on the Yale snib to double-lock it.

"There's a kettle and whatnot out the back. Why don't you brew us a cuppa while I get hold of my contact, the one I know will take the goods without asking questions."

"The same man from before?"

"Yep. Seems we're made of strong stuff, seeing as we're all still alive." He chuckled. "Although no one tells you quite how often your back goes when you're older, do they. I've suffered with mine for a few years now."

She didn't bother returning the small talk and instead went into the little room. Making tea gave her a chance to breathe, to tell herself this was all over bar Ulysses and Quenton being missing and the police trying to find where they were. She suspected the manor would stink of bleach or something similar, and they'd know Quenton going missing wasn't just a simple case of an old man walking out of his posh house and disappearing, or that he'd been kidnapped and a ransom note was imminent.

She still risked being questioned—someone could have seen her car out that way. But she was so tired, the secrets she'd harboured had become too weighty, and to be honest, she'd had enough of living on a knife edge. Not that it meant she'd confess or anything. She'd lie about everything until her dying day, but she just wanted it to come to a proper end so she could relax.

But maybe she never would. Maybe she was destined to feel uneasy forever. Her price to pay for her part in this mess.

She took a mug out to Pinocchio, who was on the phone, then trudged back into the room, sitting with her hands around her own mug, guilt prodding at her because she hadn't taken Lucia's mobile back to her yet. She'd driven to Margate last night, stayed in the caravan for a few hours' of restless sleep, then returned to London, and before driving to Essex, she'd nipped home for a wee, telling a questioning Roger she'd dropped Lucia at Haven. He'd come out into his front garden under the guise of collecting cat shit from the gravel border. A likely story.

She was knackered and already looked forward to her bed, but there was no rest for the wicked. She still had to drive to London, pop to collect Lucia from wherever the twins instructed Nora to be.

Pinocchio came in and pulled out a folding chair. He flipped it open and sat. "All sorted. He's coming to collect in an hour, so you'd best be gone by then. He won't want an audience."

Nora blurted, "I've done some bad things."

He huffed out a laugh. "Haven't we all."

"People are dead because of me. I could blame it all on my husband—he's dead an' all—but I've come to realise *I* made those decisions, regardless of what he did to put me in a certain situation, so it's *my* fault. I could have gone down a different path. All right, I wouldn't have had all that money, but I'd have had peace of mind. Funny how it takes getting older to be okay with taking the blame."

"It's called seeing things in black and white instead of all the greys and colours muddying the water. In some respects it's shit, but in others, yeah, I get what you're saying. But what's done is done, you can't change it, so you just take that money and spend it wisely, *carefully*, and try to get on with the rest of your days." He sipped his tea. "You were one of the four masked 'men', weren't you."

She didn't answer. He'd already guessed the truth of it, so what was the point? Otherwise, why would she have had the rubies and diamonds?

He sniffed. "And Goosemoor hasn't gone missing, has he."

"No. I didn't kill him, someone else did, but I was there."

"You're lucky I've got shedloads of secrets stacked up in here, that I'm not a blabber." He tapped the side of his head. "You shouldn't trust just anyone with your shit, love. Talk to me, by all means, but otherwise, keep it to yourself, eh?"

She nodded. "I don't even know why I talked about it with you."

"The burden probably got too heavy. And speaking to a stranger—or someone you don't know well—is sometimes easier. If it makes you feel better, I'll tell you a little story, then we're even. Before I set this place up, I needed cash to lease the place. I hung around with the bloke who's buying the gear you brought today, and he's…let's just say I don't know how he's never spent a day in prison, considering what he gets up to. Armed robber, fucking nutter. So I went out on a job with him. We broke into this fancy house belonging to…actually, no need to say who it belonged to. We nicked all sorts, paintings, vases, you name it, and the amount I ended up with once it had all been fenced… I didn't need to work, put it that way. But I still opened this place. Word got round on the quiet that I took goods most people wouldn't, and it's been used by the criminal fraternity ever since." He smiled. "So we've both done bad things. I've been associated with murder just by taking the gear nicked from robberies, so you're not alone—the bloke we stole from topped himself. Think we scared him a bit too much. We did what we did, and we have to live with it."

She felt better knowing she wasn't the only arsehole in the room, although she still worried about getting caught. She told him so.

"What assets have you got at your disposal?" he asked.

"Two houses, the cash from today."

"How much would you get for the houses?"

"A fair old whack, but I've got tenants in one of them."

"Then send them two months' notice to leave. Sell them. Fuck off. Get the hell away. A new life means a new person. Yeah, you'll still lug all your shit around with you inside your head, but it won't be at the forefront. Better yet, you can pay me five hundred to go and stay in my Spanish villa for a week or two. See how you feel when you're in another country. If you like it, move over there. Pack up and go."

"How come you've got a villa?"

"You might want to ask how come I've got a fake passport an' all. It cost me a ruddy packet, but it's as near perfect as a proper one, and it got me through the security checks the last three times I tested it. But I've got the villa in the same name, just in case…you know, in case someone here grasses me up for what I do."

The idea of flying away was as tempting as it was scary, but did she want to continue to go stale in the little house she'd spent the majority of her life in? Hadn't she always wanted to go abroad and see another part of the world?

"Where do I get a passport like that?"

He smiled. "I'll sort it for you, for a price. Make contact an' all that. I'll need passport photos done, obviously."

He named the amount he'd need, and Nora took it out of an envelope and passed it over.

A big sigh left him. "I might just do the same, piss off for good. Go and live in the villa full-time before it gets to the point I'd need to panic. I do like a bit of sun."

They talked for a while longer, and he made the possibility of running away sound so tempting and easy. Maybe she could persuade Lucia to go with her. She'd promised to share the ruby money, so her friend would have some to live off.

Nora left the shop to get passport photos taken with a spring in her step; she'd nip them back to Pinocchio and let his friend do the business.

She was going to become plain old Ethel Smith, a spinster.

She was going to be free.

In the BMW in the rear car park of the Noodle and Tiger, Nora sat in the back with Lucia who had clothes on that were decidedly too young for her, but then again, Nora checked herself. Who was to say that older people had to wear 'old people' clothes, all that polyester shit? Why couldn't they still be trendy in jeans and T-shirts? Just because they had drab greying hair didn't meant their wardrobe had to be just as drab.

Sod it, I'm going to buy some new clobber.

Nora had announced that she was moving to Spain, and since everyone gawped at her, she went on with, "If Lucia wants, can she come with me? Not that she needs your permission to leave her job and actually live her life, but you know what I mean."

From the passenger seat, George sighed. "It'll be hard to find a better cook than you, Lucia, but I'm sure we'll manage on that score. It's the trusting someone with the secrets that that will pose a problem. Still, not your issue."

Lucia bit her lip. "I don't know. Starting again is such a big thing. And what about my kids?"

"Free holidays bar their flights," Greg said. "They're grown-ups, I'm sure they can manage on their own, and the grandchildren will love a bit of sun every summer. Fuck knows we barely get any here. I'm surprised kids these days even know what it is."

Lucia took a deep breath. "Fuck it, I'll do it."

Nora still had half of the ruby-and-diamond payment to give her, but that was best done in private. "You'll be okay for money. You've still got the cash from the sale of your house before you moved into Haven." She gave her friend a pointed look and elbowed her knowingly. "And I'll be selling my houses. We'll get a cheap apartment each over there for half what one of my gaffs sells for."

They chatted for a while longer, discussing how long the house sales would take, plus the buying of the apartments. They reckoned within a few months, Nora and Lucia would be spending the rest of their lives in Spain.

At last, life didn't seem full of prickles just waiting for her to bleed.

Chapter Twenty-Seven

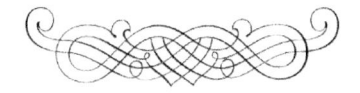

Lucia's last day at Haven had arrived. She was staying at a Premier Inn with Nora tonight, their final sleep on British soil. The July sun slanted through the window to her right, warming her hands. She'd miss this place with its constant stream of abused coming to stay, broken when they arrived, patched together by love, care, and Vic's therapy when they left. The twins had done such a good thing by opening the refuge, and she'd loved her time here.

She and Nora had gone to stay at Pinocchio's villa in May for a week, looking round for nice areas to buy apartments and getting a feel for the place. Pinocchio had sold up and moved over permanently in June, and in him they'd found a good friend, much to Lucia's surprise.

She fancied him a bit, but she hadn't told anyone that.

She peeled potatoes. It was sausage and mash tonight, garden peas or beans, and for pudding she'd made a going-away cake, three tiers with chocolate butter icing, Maltesers and crushed Flakes on top. Twelve women lived here now, so the cake wouldn't go far, not with half of them having kids with them who'd likely want more than one slice each.

She chopped the spuds in half, listening to two women talking. They all knew this was a safe space to chat, even if the words that came out of their mouths were ugly and full of vitriol at the minute. It took most of them time to leave behind their hatred and let happiness back in. They were aware the twins ran the place, and all had agreed to keep that a secret—if they didn't, they knew what they'd face.

Vicky and Alice, two of those with no children, sat at one of the tables behind Lucia. Vicky had lived here for a month, Alice for two. Lucia had picked up the gist of what Vicky had in mind, and really, Lucia ought to let the twins know, but she was so sick of shit, so sick of the bad things in life, that she was going to keep her trap shut. She was off on a plane tomorrow, and it couldn't come soon enough.

"You should tell The Brothers," Alice said. "They've already told us they'll warn off all our blokes if we want. All we've got to do is ask."

After the fiasco of killing the last lot of abusers, George and Greg had settled for only beating the shit out of them now. A sensible decision, because all those dead bodies turning up or men disappearing was going to look suspicious if it kept happening.

She'd seen the news and had put two and two together, definitely coming up with four. The copper who'd gone on a killing spree had murdered five men, and four of them had been the ones who'd abused women who'd lived at Haven. Lucia had wondered why they'd moved into new flats in a rush prior to the spree, but she'd had her query answered by that news article.

Still, that was in the past as much as Lucia's own shit was, and it could bloody well stay there.

"But they won't kill them," Vicky said. "And I want Parker dead, and I'll be the one to kill him. He doesn't deserve to live after what he put me through. I've got a permanent fucking limp, for God's sake."

Lucia could see her point. Certain men had a way of getting under your skin so you found it hard to breathe, to put one foot in front of the other in order to get through life. She should know, Quenton had done that to her—mainly his order to Nora, which had resulted in deaths that Lucia had seen in too many bad dreams on too many nights to count. They'd still occur, she didn't think moving to Spain was going to stop her subconscious from piping up, but yes, she understood that need to kill.

"I've done it," she blurted. "Killed someone." She turned to look at the women, a knife in one hand, a potato in the other. "If you're going to do it, make sure you can live with yourselves afterwards. Guilt has a nasty habit of coming to bite you in the arse."

She returned to preparing dinner, Vicky and Alice now whispering instead of talking loudly.

"Don't worry, I'm not about to tell anyone, so you can pack in that whispering," Lucia said. "And I'm leaving tonight anyway, running from what I did. I'd advise you to think long and hard about any decisions."

"I'm not about to go into it half-cocked," Vicky snapped.

Lucia wanted to tell them that with age came wisdom and experience, but she decided not to bother. People Vicky's age thought they knew it all. Fuck, Lucia had when she'd been in her twenties, too.

"It's just a bit of friendly advice," Lucia said. "Take it or leave it, it's no skin off my nose."

And actually, what the fuck do I care whether you muck it up?

She popped the potatoes in a saucepan, thinking about the all-inclusive hotel they were going to stay at in Spain while their apartments got a fresh coat of paint inside. Then there was the furniture being delivered, the lovely potted plants for their balconies. Excitement waited just around the corner.

"Fucking old cow," Vicky muttered. "I'll kill whoever I want, thanks, so keep your hooter out of it."

A part of Lucia didn't wish Vicky well, when she should—the woman had been to hell and back, according to her story—but the massive chip on her shoulder really did need to be taken off. She wasn't the most pleasant of people. Hardly surprising, given what she'd endured, but even going to see the twins' therapist hadn't shaved off her rough and spiky edges.

"I'm old to you, granted, but I'm not deaf." Lucia carried the pan over to the sink to fill it with cold water. "One more bit of advice. Suffocation is the best method. Believe me, when you smell a shedload of blood, it does something to you. Fucks with your head."

She put the pan on the hob. Lit the gas.

"Thanks," Alice said. "Sorry about Vicky, she's just a bit prickly."

"Don't speak for me," Vicky barked. "He used to do that, and it did my head in."

Lucia rolled her eyes towards the ceiling.

Good luck dealing with her, Alice, love. She's a right little madam.

Lucia walked out of the kitchen to take a break and went into the front room. She stared out of the window at the grounds. This place had been a lease of new life when she'd moved here. She'd retired early, then had come out of it when Sharon had offered her the job of cook, wages plus free board. But a better place beckoned, and who'd have thought it would be Quenton who'd send her on this new path?

She jumped, her stomach rolling over. A man legged it across the grass from the left, the security guard from out the front chasing him. The runner must have launched himself over the wall. All the women had to send photos of their abusers to Sharon, which were then printed out and put on a board in the office so the staff were aware of who to look out for should anyone come calling.

The runner was Vicky's husband.

Lucia rushed into the kitchen and shut the blinds in case he went round the back and spotted Vicky. She locked the door and turned to the women at the table, doing a mental head count—all the other women were upstairs in their rooms.

"Parker's here. Stay put and keep quiet until he's been caught."

Vicky didn't look so self-assured now, and she reached a hand up to twist her bottom lip. "Oh shit. How did he find me?"

Lucia took her phone out of her apron pocket. "I'm letting the twins know, so don't worry." She sent a message.

Fucking hell, she couldn't wait to get out of here. A job that had once seemed exciting, something to take her mind off her past, had become a burden.

But what if they went into lockdown and she wasn't allowed to leave? She'd miss her flight…

Don't be such a selfish cow.

She ran into the office. "Sharon, Parker's on the loose outside."

"Shit."

Vicky came in, shutting the door and leaning on it. "I peeked out of the window and he saw me, then fucked off over the back wall. Oh God, what have I done?"

"I told you to stay put." Lucia left the office, returning to the kitchen to wait for the potatoes to come to the boil. She wanted nothing to do with Vicky and her drama. "Watch her," she said to Alice. "She's trouble."

Alice let out a ragged breath. "I'm not getting involved with her killing him, I've told her that."

Lucia shut her eyes. "It isn't her killing him you need to worry about, it's him killing her, and if you're with her, he might go for you, too. He's found her, so she's going to have to be moved."

"Where to?"

Lucia found she didn't care. "I don't know, but take it from me, if she's let slip her location to someone, the twins aren't going to be happy."

And neither will I if I'm not gone by seven o'clock.

Thankfully, the security guard had given the all-clear, and dinner progressed as usual, George and Greg joining them. They ate the cake, everyone wishing Lucia well, and at quarter to seven, she collected her suitcases and waited for The Brothers to drop her off at the Premier Inn.

She had a change of heart just as she got out of their taxi. "Vicky's on about killing Parker, just so you know."

She wheeled her cases towards the hotel, her conscience clear on that score. What became of Parker, she'd never know, because she didn't intend to keep in contact with anyone from

London apart from her kids, their partners, and her grandchildren. Pinocchio had given her a new passport, and from now on she was Maud Green, leaving her old life behind, where it belonged.

Chapter Twenty-Eight

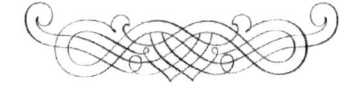

It had gone to plan, and now Vicky Hart—or should that be Kayla Barnes—would be placed in a rented flat of her own, just like she and 'Parker' had been promised would happen by the man who'd sent her to spy at Haven. Parker was really called Cooper, and he'd shaved his beard and dyed his hair blonde for the photo she'd had to send to Sharon, keeping his appearance that way for this evening's little stunt. Normally, he was black-haired. She'd bought a red wig, didn't bother with any slap, and wore glasses, shitting herself at first that the twins would recognise her from that time she'd lied about Phil touching her arse. They hadn't, but she'd still kept on her guard.

She didn't feel guilty about making friends with Alice under false pretences or lying to everyone about the so-called abuse she'd suffered. She'd had bloody good fun making it all up, actually, and it was so nice to be with a man who encouraged her to be a bitch. She'd met him not long after she'd lied about that bloke touching her up in the Noodle.

Kayla and Cooper needed somewhere to stay, what with her being kicked out of her rented place, Cooper selling drugs and generally being an arsehole, and now they'd have it. He'd been kipping at a mate's while she lived at Haven. The fact she'd passed on information to Alice's ex-husband, Everett, via a second phone she'd brought here with her, was part of the agreement of them getting the flat off the twins: confirm Alice lived at Haven, get as much information out of her as possible about her future plans, then Cooper would jump over the wall and create the issue of Kayla/Vicky no longer being safe so she had an excuse to leave.

But Alice wasn't safe either, not now. Everett wasn't going to let her just walk away from him. What he had planned for her should have meant Kayla refused to get involved, but she didn't follow the girl code, and she didn't give a shit *what* happened to the whiny little cow.

She'd done what she had to do in order to get what she wanted.

If that meant Alice turned up dead, so be it.

To be continued in *Roach*,
The Cardigan Estate 32

Printed in Great Britain
by Amazon